随遇而安，找到安宁与舒适，敞开心网，将烦躁与苦恼过滤。

简单生活,让我们飘逸而行,观花开花落,看云卷云舒。

许多人沉迷于对未来的幻想中。现在的生活,对他们而言,就像是未来生活的彩排。然而,生活绝非如此。事实上,任何人都不能保证自己明天仍存于世间。此刻是我们拥有的唯一时间,也是唯一能控制的时间。当我们的注意力集中于此刻时,就会将恐惧抛至脑后。

Simplify Your Life
简单生活

方雪梅 编译

天津教育出版社
TIANJIN EDUCATION PRESS

图书在版编目(CIP)数据

简单生活：汉英对照/方雪梅编译.—天津：天津教育出版社,2007.10
(美丽英文.第2辑)
ISBN 978-7-5309-5034-0
I.简… II.方… III.①英语—汉语—对照读物
　　　　　　　②散文—作品集—世界
　　　　　　　③随笔—作品集—世界 IV.H319.4: I
中国版本图书馆 CIP 数据核字(2007)第 159110 号

简单生活

出版人	肖占鹏
责任编辑	匡　威
装帧设计	飞鸟工作室

作　者	方雪梅　编译
出版发行	天津教育出版社
	天津市和平区西康路 35 号
	邮政编码　300051
经　销	新华书店
印　刷	北京中印联印务有限公司
版　次	2007 年 11 月第 1 版
印　次	2007 年 11 月第 1 次
规　格	16 开（720×1000 毫米）
字　数	300 千字
印　张	14
书　号	ISBN 978-7-5309-5034-0
定　价	19.80 元

目录 CONTENTS

第一卷 学会生活在此时此刻
Learn to Live in the Present Moment

热爱生活	2
Love Your Life	3
工作和娱乐	4
Work and Pleasure	5
想想好事情	6
Try to Remember the Good Things	7
活出个性	8
An Identity of One's Own	9
让自己轻松一刻	10
Give Yourself a Break	11
清理心灵空间	12
Clear Your Mental Space	14
品味现在	16
Relish the Moment	17
学会生活在此时此刻	18
Learn to Live in the Present Moment	19
无知常乐	20
Ignorance Make One Happy	21
美丽人生	22
Beauty	24
做你自己	26
Do Things for Himself	27

人生就是要自在逍遥地与自然和谐相处。

多想想你所拥有的，你会懂得心满意足的含义。

论闲散	28
On Idleness	30
过平静生活的代价是什么	33
What Is the Price of Personal Peace	35
充满活力愉快地生活	37
To Be Full of Energy, Joy and Life	38
阴郁的日子	39
The Blue Day	41
感触美丽	43
Feeling Beauty	44
喜悦的能力	45
The Faculty of Delight	46
我喜欢这种淡淡的感觉	47
I Like the Subtle Feeling	48
飘逸而行	49
Go Easy and Enjoy Yourself in Harmony	50
就为了今天	51
Just for Today	52
想想你所拥有的	53
Think More about What You Have	54
自由飞翔	55
Free to Soar	56
彼岸无尽头，知足才常乐	57
"There" Is No Better Than "Here"	59

目录 CONTENTS

第二卷 别让快乐远离我们
Don't Let Happiness Run Away From Us

自由如歌的快乐	62
On Pleasure	64
幸福之道	66
The Road to Happiness	68
快乐之门	70
The Happy Door	71
做一个乐观者	72
Be an Optimist	74
我们对幸福的追求	76
Our Pursuit of Happiness	78
别让快乐远离我们	80
Don't Let Happiness Run Away From Us	81
感受快乐	82
Ten Ways to Happiness	83
幸福的真谛	84
The Essence of Happiness	86
生活的乐趣	88
The Joy of Living	89
排遣压力,享受生活	90
12 Ways to Minimize Stress	92
幸福生活的建议	94
Good Advice to Help You Live Happily	96

保持快乐的心境是一种成就,是灵魂与性格的升华。

生命是一样既抽象又具体的东西，让人既畏惧又渴望。

金钱能买到幸福吗	98
Does Money Buy Happiness	100
我们在享受快乐吗	102
Are We Having Fun Yet	104
幸　福	106
Happiness	107
选择乐观	108
Choose Optimism	110
快乐真言	112
A Simple Truth about Happiness	114
快乐法则	116
Five Simple Rules	118
幸福是一种感觉	120
Blessed	121
幸福箴言	122
On Happiness	123
请喝杯茶	124
A Cup of Tea	125
步行的乐趣	126
The Pleasure of Walking	127
幸福就在我们身边	128
Happiness Is All Around Us	129
幸福在哪里	130
Where Is Happiness	131

第三卷 生活是一所全日制学校
A Full-time School Called Life

生命的启示	134
Instructions for Life	136
感悟生活	138
Word of Wisdom	139
生命	140
Life	141
人生絮语	142
Moving Thoughts	144
平和的心态	146
A Good Measure of Equanimity	147
我的生活真的那么糟吗	148
Is My Life Real Bad	149
生活给我上的一课	150
A Lesson of Life	152
体验生活	154
Experience Life	156
草草行事的重要性	158
The Importance of Doing Things Badly	162
做自己情绪的主人	167
Today I Will be Master of My Emotions	169
让内心的灯指引你	171

幸福不是发生在我们周围的事,而是我们如何看待周围发生的事。

只要你选择了触动他人的心灵，这些选择便是生活的全部。

Allow Your Own Inner Light to Guide You	172
保持平静小贴士	173
Tips for Staying Calm	176
论宁静的心境	179
On Peace of Mind	180
生活是一所全日制学校	181
A Full-time School Called Life	183
一生的收获	185
Catch of a Lifetime	187
生　活	189
Life	191
生活的课堂	193
A Lesson in Life	194
人生之道	195
For Success in Life	196
和自己交谈的力量	197
Power of Self-talk	199
重新定义自己	201
Redefine Yourself	203
聆听心灵	205
Listen to Your Inner Voice	206
打造自己的生活	207
How to Build Your Life	209
生活半对半	211
The 50-Percent Theory of Life	213

第一卷

学会生活在此时此刻

Learn to Live in the Present Moment

战胜恐惧最好的策略是,学会将注意力转回现在的每时每刻。许多人沉迷于对未来的幻想中。现在的生活,对他们而言,就像是未来生活的彩排。然而,生活绝非如此。事实上,任何人都不能保证自己明天仍存于世间。此刻是我们拥有的唯一时间,也是唯一能控制的时间。当我们的注意力集中于此刻时,就会将恐惧抛至脑后。

热爱生活

亨利·大卫·梭罗

　　无论生活如何卑微,你都应勇敢地面对它,不要躲避它,也不要诅咒它。其实生活并不像你想象的那么糟。你最富有的时候,它反而最贫瘠。吹毛求疵的人,天堂也能被他挑出毛病。即便你的生活是贫穷的,也要热爱它。快活、激动和光荣的时光甚至在济贫院里也享受得到。夕阳照射在贫民居所的窗户上所反射的光同照在富人公寓的窗户上所反射的光一样耀眼夺目,都能使得门前的积雪在早春消融。虽然我没有亲见,但我可以感知到,济贫院里的人们一定是从容地、心满意足地生活着,犹如生活在宫殿中一般幸福快乐。在我看来,小镇上的穷人往往活得最为独立自在。或许是因为他们不必为是否要接受什么而劳神费力吧。不要自找麻烦地去追求新鲜事物,新衣物和新朋友。让旧物常新,回归旧物。万物不变,是我们在变。衣服可以卖掉,但要永存思想。

心灵小语

　　人们都在为生活忙碌着,很多人都认为生活很艰难,甚至不愿活在这个世上。难道生活真的那么恐怖吗?其实还在于人们对它的看法。不管你的生活多么卑微,勇敢地面对,不可逃避,不可报以恶言。生活并不是可怕的怪兽,我们应该用微笑来面对它。跟它握握手吧,它会欣然接受的!

Love Your Life

Henry David Thoreau

However mean your life is, meet it and live it; do not shun it and call it hard names. It is not so bad as you are. It looks poorest when you are richest. The fault-finder will find faults in **paradise**[1]. Love your life, poor as it is. You may perhaps have some pleasant, thrilling, glorious hours, even in a poor-house. The setting sun is reflected from the windows of the **alms-house**[2] as brightly as from the rich man's **abode**[3]; the snow melts before its door as early in the spring. I do not see but a quiet mind may live as contentedly there, and have as cheering thoughts, as in a palace. The town's poor seem to me often to live the most **independent**[4] lives of any. Maybe they are simply great enough to receive without misgiving. Do not trouble yourself much to get new things, whether clothes or friends. Turn the old, return to them. Things do not change; we change. Sell your clothes and keep your thoughts.

热词空间

1. paradise ['pærədaiz] *n.* 天堂
2. alms-house *n.* 救济院
3. abode [ə'bəud] *n.* 房屋；居所
4. independent [indi'pendənt] *adj.* 独立自主的；不受约束的

工作和娱乐

温斯顿·伦纳德·斯宾塞·丘吉尔

　　想要获得真正的幸福与平安,一个人至少应该有两三种业余爱好,而且必须是真正的爱好。到了晚年才开始说"我对什么什么感兴趣"是毫无益处的,这样的尝试只会增加精神上的负担。在与自己日常工作无关的某些领域中,一个人可以获得渊博的知识,但他几乎得不到实在的益处或放松。喜欢干什么就干什么是无益的,你得干一行爱一行。广义而言,人类可以分成三个阶层:劳累而死的人、忧虑而死的人和烦恼而死的人。对于那些体力劳动者来说,在经过一周精疲力竭的工作之后,周六下午给他们提供踢足球或打棒球的机会是没有意义的。对于政界人士、专业人士或商人来说,他们已为棘手的事务操劳或烦恼了六天,在周末再请他们为琐事劳神,同样是毫无意义的。

　　或者可以这么说,理智的、勤奋的、有用的人可以分为两类:第一类,他们的工作就是工作,娱乐就是娱乐;第二类,他们的工作和娱乐是合二为一的。当然,很大一部分人都属于第一类人。他们可以得到相应的补偿。在办公室或工厂里长时间地工作,带给他们的不仅是维持生计的金钱,还带给他们一种渴求娱乐的强烈欲望,哪怕是最简单、最朴实的娱乐方式。命运的宠儿则属于第二类人。他们的生活自然而和谐。在他们看来,工作时间永远不够多,每一天在他们看来都是假期;而当正常的假期到来时,他们总会抱怨他们正在倾心投入的休假被强行中断了。然而,有一些东西对于这两类人来说是十分必要的,那就是变换一下视角,改变一下氛围,努力做一件别的事情。事实上,每隔一段时间,那些把工作看成娱乐的人们很可能最需要以某种方式把工作驱赶出他们的大脑。

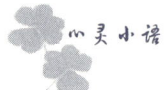

　　本文将人们对工作和娱乐的看法分为两类,一是界限分明,二是合二为一,我们属于哪类人,应该属于哪类人,或是我们哪类都不应属于!

Work and Pleasure

Winston Leonard Spencer Churchill

To be really happy and really safe, one ought to have at least two or three hobbies, and they must all be real. It is no use starting late in life to say: "I will take an interest in this or that." Such an attempt only aggravates the strain of mental effort. A man may acquire great knowledge of topics unconnected with his daily work, and yet hardly get any benefit or relief. It is no use doing what you like; you have got to like what you do. Broadly speaking, human beings may be divided into three classes: those who are toiled to death, those who are worried to death, and those who are bored to death. It is no use offering the manual labourer, tired out with a hard week's sweat and effort, the chance of playing a game of football or baseball on Saturday afternoon. It is no use inviting the politician or the professional or business man, who has been working or worrying about serious things for six days, to work or worry about trifling things at the weekend.

It may also be said that rational, industrious, useful human beings are divided into two classes: first, those whose work is work and whose pleasure is pleasure; and secondly, those whose work and pleasure are one. Of these the former are the majority. They have their compensations. The long hours in the office or the factory bring with them as their reward, not only the means of sustenance, but a keen appetite for pleasure even in its simplest and most modest forms. But Fortune's favoured children belong to the second class. Their life is a natural harmony. For them the working hours are never long enough. Each day is a holiday, and ordinary holidays when they come are grudged as enforced interruptions in an absorbing vocation. Yet to both classes the need of an alternative outlook, of a change of atmosphere, of a diversion of effort, is essential. Indeed, it may well be that those whose work is their pleasure are those who most need the means of banishing it at intervals from their minds.

想想好事情

佚名

不经意间我们会身处逆境,那么请追忆生命中那些充满快乐与幸福的时光吧!

追忆它如何将快乐赐予你,于是你便勇气倍增,生活中的难题也将迎刃而解。

在重重困难面前举步维艰时,回想你努力奋斗最终取得胜利的时刻。

那样,不管生活如何艰难,我们都可坦然而过。

当你觉得身心疲惫时,寻找一个心灵憩息之所,让自己得以片刻休息。

要给自己留点时间去梦想,去充电,以全新的自我迎接未来的一天。

当你感觉心中的弦崩得太紧时,去找点有趣的事做做。如此,你的压力便渐渐消失,而你的想法也渐趋明朗。

当困难接踵而至时,要明白,就生命的整个历程而言,这些困难犹如空气中的尘埃无足轻重——想想好事情。

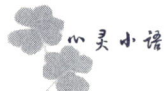

每个人都会遇到艰难和困苦,担心和恐惧无疑是火上添油,那我们又该怎样面对和解决它呢?"想想好事情"或许会是一个好方法,它会给我们的精神带来巨大的慰藉,使我们能够鼓起勇气并坚定信念。身处逆境时,寻找一个寂静之地,回忆从前美好的种种,使我们的心绪得以解脱,从而轻松地面对一切!

Try to Remember the Good Things

Anonymous

When times become difficult (and you know they sometimes will), remember a moment in your life that was filled with joy and happiness.

Remember how it made you feel, and you will have the strength you need to get through any **trial**[1].

When life throws you one more obstacle than you think you can handle, remember something you achieved through perseverance and by struggling to the end.

In doing so, you'll find you have the ability to overcome each **obstacle**[2] brought your way.

When you find yourself drained and depleted of energy, remember to find a place of **sanctuary**[3] and rest.

Take the necessary time in your own life to dream your dreams and renew your energy, so you'll be ready to face each new day.

When you feel tension building, find something fun to do. You'll find that the stress you feel will **dissipate**[4] and your thoughts will become clearer.

When you're faced with so many negative and draining situations, realize how minuscule problems will seem when you view your life as a whole—and remember the positive things.

热词空间

1. trial ['traiəl] n. 试验;考验;审讯;审判
2. obstacle ['ɔbstəkl] n. 障碍;妨害物
3. sanctuary ['sæŋktjuəri] n. 避难所
4. dissipate ['disipeit] v. 驱散;(使)(云、雾、疑虑等)消散;浪费(金钱或时间)

活出个性

佚名

  在浩渺的大千世界中,每个人都仅有一次生存的机会——它是无与伦比,不可挽回的。正如卢梭所说,上帝创造了你,即刻打碎了那个属于你的特定模子。

  名誉、财富、知识等仅为身外之物,并且每个人都在为获取它们而努力奋斗着。但你的人生经历和感受却是你的私人财产,无人可与你分享。你死后,也无人能替你再活一次。如果你真正意识到了这一点,你就会懂得,人生在世,活出自己的独特个性和滋味是最重要的。衡量你的人生有意义与否的标准不是外在的成功,而是你对人生意义的独特理解和感悟,从而使个性绽放异彩。

  真正做成自己并非一件易事。世间有好多人,你可以通过许多途径去识别他,他的职业,身份,社会地位等,唯独不是通过他的个性去识别。如果一个人总是按别人的意愿生活,没有自己的独立思想,总是忙于身外之物,没有自己的个性生活,那么,说他不是他自己就一点儿都不为过。因为从他的头脑到他的心灵,你确实找不到一样只属于他自己的东西,他只不过是别人的一个影子和办事的机器罢了。

  时代在发展,社会在进步,人们的个性也愈加鲜明。一句名言这样说道:世上没有相同的两片叶子。每个人都是这个世上独一无二的,都有着自己独特的优势。"跟风"只会将自己的特别之处埋没。所以,我们要活出个性,做我们自己!

An Identity of One's Own

Anonymous

In the eternal universe, every human being has a **one-off**[1] chance to live—his existence is unique and **irretrievable**[2], for the mold with which he was made, as Rousseau said, was broken by God immediately afterwards.

Fame, wealth and knowledge are merely worldly possessions that are within the reach of anybody striving for them. But your experience of and feelings about life are your own and not to be shared. No one can live your life over again after your death. A full awareness of this will point out to you that the most important thing in your existence is your distinctive individuality or something special of yours. What really counts is not your worldly success but your peculiar insight into the meaning of life and your **commitment**[3] to it, which add luster to your personality.

It is not easy to be what one really is. There is many a person in the world who can be identified as anything—either his job, his status or his social role—that shows no trace about his individuality. It does do him justice to say that he has no identity of his own, if he doesn't know his own mind and all his things are either arranged by others or done on others' suggestions; if his life, always occupied by external things, is completely void of an inner world. You won't be able to find anything whatever, from head to heart, that truly belongs to him. He is, indeed, no more than a shadow cast by somebody else or a machine capable of doing business.

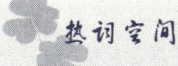

1. one-off *adj.* 仅一次
2. irretrievable [ˌiriˈtriːvəbl] *adj.* 不可挽回；不可补救的
3. commitment [kəˈmitmənt] *n.* 承诺；义务

让自己轻松一刻

佚名

没有人可以做任何事。每个人都必须做出选择,接受调整。问题是许多人都会选择将自己和健康放置最后。他们关心房子和车子,胜过他们自己。他们将别人的需求放于首位。如果是偶尔的事,那也是可以的。如果能保持平衡,那也没问题。但是许多人的那种生活方式使他们非常疲惫,感觉失控。幸运的是,生活不需要那样。

一句俗语非常有用:是索尔·高登与哈罗德·布罗舍尔合作的一本书的名字——《生活变幻莫测——吃了甜点再说》。如果好东西常常放置在最后,它们通常会消失。将工作放于健康和快乐之前,工作很快就会取代健康和快乐。

请注意它是怎样发生的:人们忙于工作,觉得时间很短;他们将锻炼和吃饭的时间省去;后来就减少休息的时间。很快,他们忙碌到没有时间去探望朋友;他们停止读书或是打球,六个月都不散步。这不是生活的好方式。

该怎样解决这种情况呢?总而言之,懂得取舍。看清你生活中想要的是什么,将其放置首位。以日常生活为基础,包括固定的膳食,足够的睡眠和与家人共处的时间。锻炼、休闲、友谊和爱好也是生活的基本方面。关键是做自己的事情:不管怎样,只要感觉自己和生活舒适就好。抽个空小睡一会、散散步、弹弹钢琴。当然,你必须将最近的许多麻烦事替换掉。不要将公文包从办公室带回家。不要将自己的房间打扫得像你母亲的房间一样洁净。将更多的时间用于你想做的事情,而不是必须做的事情。

将你的名字列入想要制造快乐的人的名单中。不要"我第一"或是"唯我独尊",而要"我也是"。平衡才是目标。许可才是关键。就从此刻开始!

现代社会的生活节奏越来越快,人们的压力也越来越大,通常会使人无法适应、情绪低迷、生活失控。所以我们要以健康的身体、愉悦的心情、积极的心态投入到工作和学习中,做到每天都心情舒畅,微笑着面对生活。

Give Yourself a Break

Anonymous

No one can do it all. Each of us has to make choices and accept trade-offs. The problem is, many people choose in ways that put themselves and their health last. They take better care of their houses and cars than they do of themselves. They put everyone else's needs ahead of their own. That's fine if it's occasional. It would even be okay if there was a balance. But most people living that way are wearing themselves out, feeling out of control. Fortunately, life doesn't have to be like that.

One phrase can be very helpful: It's the name of a book by Sol Gordon and Harold Brochure, *Life Is Uncertain—Eat Dessert First*! If the good stuff always gets left until last, it usually doesn't happen. Work before health and pleasure soon becomes work instead of health and pleasure.

Notice how it happens: Folks get busy and run short of time; they stop exercising or start skipping meals; next they steal time from their sleep. Soon they get too busy to see friends; they stop reading or playing ball, and six months go by without a long walk. That's not a great way to live.

So what is the solution? In a word, prioritize. Decide what you want in your life, and put that first. On a daily basis, that should include regular meals, adequate sleep and time with your family. Exercise, leisure, friendships and hobbies should also be regular aspects of life. The point is to do something for yourself: whatever makes you feel good about yourself and your life. Take a nap. Take a walk. Take time to play the piano. Of course, you'll have to trade off some of the things that are currently clogging your schedule to make room for your new priorities. Stop bringing your briefcase home from the office. Stop keeping your house as clean as your mother kept hers. Fill more of your time with want-to-dos instead of have-to-dos.

Add your name to the list of people who're trying to make happy. Not "me first" or "me only" but "me, too." Balance is the goal. Permission is the key. And the time to start is now.

清理心灵空间

珍妮弗·吉弗莱

回想一下你上次产生的消极情绪,如压抑、气愤或受挫。当你身处那种消极情绪中时,你的头脑里在想些什么呢?你的头脑是混乱如麻?还是瘫痪了,不能再进行思考?

下一次,当你发现自己非常压抑,或者极其愤怒或万分沮丧时,尽量停止吧。对!就是停止。无论你现在正做着什么,停止手头的工作,静坐一会儿。静坐的同时,让自己完全沉浸在消极的情绪之中。

让那种情绪完全地将你吞噬,让自己有一点时间真实地去感受那种情绪。在这里,不要欺骗自己。用整整一分钟——仅仅一分钟——不去做其他任何事情,只去感受那种情绪。

当整整一分钟过去,问问你自己:"在今天剩余的时间里,我愿意继续这种消极情绪吗?"

只要你彻底地将自己沉入其中,并真实地去体会它,你就会意外地发现那种情绪很快就消失了。

如果你觉得有必要再将这种情绪继续一段时间,那好,没关系,再给自己一分钟,去体会这种情绪。

如果你觉得自己体会得很透彻了,那就问问自己是否愿意让这种消极继续在你的剩余时间里存在。如果是"不",那就深呼吸一次,将所有的消极随着你的呼吸释放出去。

这种方法看似简单——几乎是过分地简单了,但是其效果却很显著。通过给自己真正体会消极情绪的空间,你能够真正与这种情绪接触,而不是去压抑它、回避它。给这种情绪一定的空间,给它必要的关注,这样真正使你消除了其力量。当你沉浸在这种情绪中时,就会明白它只是一种情感,就会不再受其影响。然后,你就可以清理自己的头脑,继续工作了。

试试这种方法。下一次当你处于消极的情绪之中时,让自己有体会这种情绪的一点空间,然后看看随后会发生什么。随身带着一张写着下面这些话的纸:

停止。让自己在这种情绪中沉浸一分钟。我想要这种情绪继续下去吗?深呼吸,放松,继续行动!

这张纸会提醒你要做的步骤。需要牢记的是,用必要的时间真正将自己沉浸在那种情绪之中。然后,当你认为自己充分体会这种情绪时,就将其释放——让它真正地从你的心中消失。你一定会惊讶于摆脱消极情绪和着手工作的迅速。

遇到了挫折,精神状态不好,于是情绪低迷,烦闷不安,不能专心工作,心情浮躁,想必这样的情况大家都遇到过,你是怎样克服的呢?本文就给大家建议了一个很好的方法,可以使大家从心理上打败这种消极情绪,积极投身于工作。可以尝试一下,效果很不错!

Clear Your Mental Space

Jennifer Givler

Think about the last time you felt a **negative**[1] emotion—like stress, anger, or frustration. What was going through your mind as you were going through that negativity? Was your mind cluttered with thoughts? Or was it paralyzed, unable to think?

The next time you find yourself in the middle of a very stressful time, or you feel angry or **frustrated**[2], stop. Yes, that's right, stop. Whatever you're doing, stop and sit for one minute. While you're sitting there, completely immerse yourself in the negative emotion.

Allow that emotion to consume you. Allow yourself one minute to truly feel that emotion. Don't cheat yourself here. Take the entire minute—but only one minute—to do nothing else but feel that emotion.

When the minute is over, ask yourself, "Am I willing to keep holding on to this negative emotion as I go through the rest of the day?"

Once you've allowed yourself to be totally immersed in the emotion and really feel it, you will be surprised to find that the emotion clears rather quickly.

If you feel you need to hold on to the emotion for a little longer, that is Ok. Allow yourself another minute to feel the emotion.

When you feel you've had enough of the emotion, ask yourself if you're willing to carry that negativity with you for the rest of the day. If not, take a deep breath, as you **exhale**[3], release all that negativity with your breath.

This exercise seems simple—almost too simple. But, it is very effective. By allowing that negative emotion the space to be truly felt, you are dealing with the emotion rather than stuffing it down and trying not to feel it. You are actually taking away the power of the emotion by giving it the space and attention it needs. When you immerse yourself in the emotion, and realize that it is only emotion, it loses its control. You can clear your head and proceed with your task.

Try it. Next time you're in the middle of a negative emotion, give yourself the space to feel the emotion and see what happens. Keep a piece of paper with you that say the following:

Stop. **Immerse**[4] for one minute. Do I want to keep this negativity? Breath deep, exhale, release. Move on!

This will remind you of the steps to the process. Remember, take the time you need to really immerse yourself in the emotion. Then, when you feel you've felt it enough, **release**[5] it — really let go of it. You will be surprised at how quickly you can move on from a negative situation and get to what you really want to do!

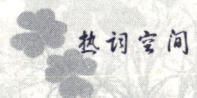

1. negative ['negətiv] *adj.* 否定的;消极的
2. frustrated [frʌ'streitid] *adj.* 失败的;落空的
3. exhale [eks'heil] *v.* 呼气;发出;发散
4. immerse [i'mə:s] *v.* 沉浸;使陷入
5. release [ri'li:s] *v.* 释放;解放;放弃

品味现在

罗伯特·J.黑斯廷斯

在我们内心深处,总隐藏着一片诗情画意的风景。我们觉得自己正处于一次跨越大陆的漫长旅行中。坐在火车上,窗外流动的风景在我们面前一掠而过:附近高速公路上驰骋的汽车;十字路口挥手的孩童;远处山坡上放牧的牛群;电厂排放的袅袅烟尘;成片的玉米地和小麦地;还有,平原、峡谷、山脉和丘陵;城市的轮廓和乡间的农舍。

可是,我们想得最多的还是目的地。某天的某一刻,我们抵达站点,会有乐队演奏,欢迎旗帜飘扬。一旦我们到达了目的地,梦想就会变成现实,而我们破碎的生活会像一幅拼好的画图,变的完美。我们焦躁不安地在车厢里踱来踱去,诅咒火车的迟缓——等啊等,等待进站的那一刻。

"进站时,一切都好了!"我们呼喊着。"我满18岁时。""我买了一辆新的450SL奔驰轿车时!""当我供最小的孩子读完大学。""当我还了所有的贷款。""当我退休的时候,就从此过上了幸福的生活!"

"品味现在"本身就是一句很好的箴言,再加上《圣经·诗篇》第118章第24行的这样一句话,使它更显特别,"主创造了今天,我们为活在今日而欢欣雀跃。"导致人们疯狂的往往不是今日的沉重,而是对昨日的懊悔和对明日的畏惧。懊悔和畏惧如同一对孪生的窃贼,偷走了我们的今天。

因此,别再在车厢内徘徊,不要再计算着余下的行程吧!让我们攀登更多的高山,吃冰淇淋、赤脚漫步、游泳、欣赏日落、多点欢笑、少些泪水吧。让生命活在我们前进的脚步中,那么车站很快就会到达。

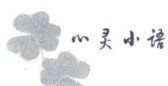

本文的作者将生命比作一次旅行,每一个生活目标都是一个站点,并总是焦虑地等待下一个站点,希望能有意外的收获,可是时光流逝,最终发现生命没有终点!

Relish the Moment

Robert J. Hastings

Tucked away in our subconsciousness is an idyllic vision. We see ourselves on a long trip that spans the continent. We are traveling by train. Out the windows, we drink in the passing scene of cars on nearby highways, of children waving at a crossing, of cattle grazing on a distant hillside, of smoke pouring from a power plant, of row upon row of corn and wheat, of flatlands and valleys, of mountains and rolling hillsides, of city skylines and village halls.

But uppermost in our minds is the final destination. On a certain day at a certain hour, we will pull into the station. Bands will be playing and flags waving. Once we get there, so many wonderful dreams will come true and the pieces of our lives will fit together like a completed jigsaw puzzle. How restlessly we pace the aisles, damning the minutes for loitering—waiting, waiting, waiting for the station.

"When we reach the station, that will be it!" we cry. "When I'm 18." "When I buy a new 450SL Mercedes Benz!" "When I put the last kid through college." "When I have paid off the mortgage!" "When I get a promotion." "When I reach the age of retirement, I shall live happily ever after!"

"Relish the moment" is a good motto, especially when coupled with Psalm 118:24: "This is the day which the Lord hath made; we will rejoice and be glad in it." It isn't the burdens of today that drive men mad. It is the regrets over yesterday and the fear of tomorrow. Regret and fear are twin thieves who rob us of today.

So stop pacing the aisles and counting the miles. Intend, climb more mountains, eat more ice cream, go barefoot more often, swim more rivers, watch more sunsets, laugh more, cry less. Life must be lived as we go along. The station will come soon enough.

学会生活在此时此刻

理查德·卡里森

在很大程度上,能不能生活在此时此刻,是衡量我们内心世界是否平和的一个标准。不论昨日或去年发生了什么,也不管将会发生什么,此刻才是我们的真正所在——并且始终都是!

诚然,许多人把生命耗费在焦虑之中,我们同时对一连串的事情忧心,因此而导致的神经过敏几乎成了一种我们熟稔的艺术。对过去的困惑和对未来的忧虑占据了我们当前的每时每刻。于是,我们整日忧心忡忡,灰心丧气,情绪低落,甚至悲观绝望。另一方面,我们不断推让自己获得满足感的时间,推延应当优先考虑的事,推后自己的幸福感,并常用最有力的理由说服自己,"有一天"将会比今天更加美好。遗憾的是,如此期待未来的精神安慰只会周而复始地重复。所以,"有一天"永远都不会真正到来。约翰·列农曾经说过,"生活就是我们忙于制定其他计划时所发生的一切。"当我们正制定"其他的计划"时,孩子们正迅速地成长,爱人或离开或死亡。我们的身体开始变形,梦想开始消逝。总之,我们正失去生活。

许多人沉迷于对未来的幻想中。现在的生活,对他们而言,就像是未来生活的彩排。然而,生活绝非如此。事实上,任何人都不能保证自己明天仍存于世间。此刻是我们拥有的唯一时间,也是唯一能控制的时间。当我们的注意力集中于此刻时,就会将恐惧抛至脑后。恐惧是我们对未来可能发生之事的忧虑——我们没有足够的钱,我们的孩子会陷入麻烦,我们会变老甚至死亡,等等。

战胜恐惧最好的策略是,学会将注意力转回现在的每时每刻。马克·吐温说过,"我一生经历过许多恐怖的事,但有一些纯粹是偶然。"我想,没有比这说得更好的了。把你的注意力集中在此时此刻,你的付出终将有硕果回报。

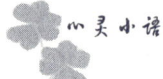

有许多人在为过去的过错懊悔,可是我们不应总是停留在过去;展望未来是好事,可是不应一味将希望寄托于明天。懂得把握今天的人,才是真正懂得生活的人

Learn to Live in the Present Moment

Richard Carison

To a large degree, the measure of our peace of mind is determined by how much we are able to live in the present moment. Irrespective of what happened yesterday or last year, and what may or may not happen tomorrow, the present moment is where you are—always!

Without question, many of us have mastered the neurotic art of spending much of our lives worrying about a variety of things—all at once. We allow past problems and future concerns to dominate our present moments, so much so that we end up anxious, frustrated, depressed, and hopeless. On the flip side, we also postpone our gratification, our stated priorities, and our happiness, often convincing ourselves that "someday" will be better than today. Unfortunately, the same mental dynamics that tell us to look toward the future will only repeat themselves so that "someday" never actually arrives. John Lennon once said, "Life is what's happening while we're busy making other plans." When we're busy making "other plans", our children are busy growing up, and people we love are moving away and dying, our bodies are getting out of shape, and our dreams are slipping away. In short, we miss out on life.

Many people live as if life were a dress rehearsal for some later date. It isn't. In fact, no one has a guarantee that he or she will be here tomorrow. Now is the only time we have, and the only time that we have any control over. When our attention is in the present moment, we push fear from our minds. Fear is the concern over events that might happen in the future—we won't have enough money, our children will get into trouble, we will get old and die, whatever.

To combat fear, the best strategy is to learn to bring your attention back to the present. Mark Twain said, "I have been through some terrible things in my life, some of which actually happened." I don't think I can say it any better. Practice keeping your attention on the here and now. Your efforts will pay great dividends.

无知常乐

罗伯特·林德

普通人只会使用电话,却无法解释电话的工作原理。他把电话、火车、铸造排字机、飞机都看作自然而然的事情。对于这些事,他既不产生怀疑,也不去了解。我们每个人真正下工夫去了解、弄清楚的似乎只是很小范围内的某几件事。大多数人把日常工作以外的一切知识都当成花哨无用的东西。然而,我们还是时时抗拒着我们的无知。我们有时也会清醒起来,进行思索。我们信手拈来一个什么题目,思考它,甚至入迷——关于死后的生命,或者关于某些据说亚里士多德也迷惑不解的问题,例如,"打喷嚏,从中午到子夜则吉,从子夜至中午则凶,是什么原因呢?"为求知识而陷入无知,这是人类所欣赏的最大乐事之一。归根结底,无知的最大快乐在于提出问题。一个人如果丧失了这种提问的快乐,或者把它换成了教条的答案,并且以此为乐,那么,他的头脑已经开始僵化了。朱厄尔这样勤学好问的人是我们所羡慕的,他到了六十多岁居然还能坐下来研究生理学。我们大多数人还没到他这么大的岁数就早已不再有自己无知的感觉了。我们甚至对自己一点浅薄的知识感到沾沾自喜,而把与日俱增的年龄看成是通向无所不知的天然学堂。我们忘记了:苏格拉底因智慧而名垂后世,并不是因为他无所不知,而是因为他在70岁高龄时还明白自己依然一无所知。

作者定义的"无知常乐"并不是指一无所知的我们会感到开心和幸福,而是指我们在不懂情况下,要提出问题,寻求答案,从而享受这种求知的快乐。就连苏格拉底这样以智慧著称的圣人,也觉得自己需要继续求知。朋友,让我们在"无知"中发问,充分享受这过程中的快乐吧!

Ignorance Make One Happy

Robert Lynd

The average man who uses a telephone could not explain how a telephone works. He takes for granted the telephone, the railway train, the linotype, the airplane. He neither questions nor understands them. It is as though each of us investigated and made his own only a tiny circle of facts. Knowledge outside the day's work is regarded by most men as a **gewgaw**[1]. Still we are constantly in reaction against our ignorance. We rouse ourselves at intervals and speculate. We revel in speculations about anything at all—about life after death or about such questions as that which is said to have puzzled Aristotle, "why sneezing from noon to midnight was good, but from night to noon unlucky." One of the greatest joys known to man is to take such a flight into ignorance in search of knowledge. The great pleasure of ignorance is, after all, the pleasure of asking questions. The man who has lost this pleasure or exchanged it for the pleasure of **dogma**[2], which is the pleasure of answering, is already beginning to **stiffen**[3]. One envies so inquisitive a man as Jewell, who sat down to the study of physiology in his sixties. Most of us have lost the sense of our ignorance long before that age. We even become vain of our squirrel's hoard of knowledge and regard increasing age itself as a school of omniscience. We forget that Socrates was famed for wisdom not because he was omniscient but because he realized at the age of seventy that he still knew nothing.

1. gewgaw ['gjuːgɔː] *n.* 华而不实的东西
2. dogma ['dɔgmə] *n.* 教义；教条
3. stiffen ['stifn] *v.* 使硬；变硬；变猛烈

美丽人生

佚名

她有一种外表无法诠释的聪颖和秀美。她的声音正是我们所要聆听的那种,她的言语能轻易地进驻人们的心灵。

据说人生的真谛是无以言说的。言语的阐述、艺术的表达,还有人类那似乎永无休止的错综复杂的思考,三者的目的都是在追求人生的真谛。希望接近,甚至是完全把握人生存在的意义,这可以使人近乎痴狂。偶尔有人会坚信真理,并以之为自己的志趣,追求真理重于保全生命,于是就有了舍身而取义的壮举。然而,也有另一种人生,即在追求真理的过程中润泽生命。

过去我常会在教堂的心意篮中发现一些短小精悍的美文,一些是有关我的布道,还有一些是作者平时读《圣经》的感想。写这些短文的人不仅反思了我的某些观点,同时还引用了一些他/她曾读过的,他/她所喜爱的诗人或神秘主义者那些令人难忘的话语。这些短文深深吸引了我。我看到了一个执著追求真与美的人。这些珍藏的话语优美且感人。我有种感觉,这些字句好像很高兴被我们发现,它们如此慷慨地毫无保留地为无名作者所用,而今轮到这位无名氏来学习与人分享这些美文的奥秘了。这样的分享使美愈加生辉。事实上,世上唯一的真理是可免费索取的。

很久以后我才看到这些美文的作者。

一个周日早上,我被告知办公室有人等我。给我应门的年轻人说"是个女士,她说留言是她放的。"见到她时我不禁大吃一惊,因为我一下子就认出了她是我教区的信徒,只是我始终不知道那些美文是出自她手。她坐在椅子上,双手相握放在大腿上,头低垂着。她抬头看我时,微笑起来却十分费力。那是一张被毁了容的脸,外科手术使她的脸皮紧绷,笑对她来说是非常困难的事儿。为了去除脸上碍眼的肉瘤,她接受了令人痛苦的手术治疗。

那个周日早上我们聊了一会儿,并商量好那周再找个时间共进午餐。

而后我们不止吃了一顿午饭,而是吃了好多顿。每次她都头戴帽子。我想或许是某种治疗使她脱了好多发。我们将各自生活中的点点滴滴讲出来一起分享。我向她讲述了我读书和成长的故事。她告诉我她在一家保险公司工作了好多年。但她从未提及她的家庭，我也就没过问。

我们还谈及了大家都读过的一些文章的作者，显然她是一个酷爱读书的人。

这些年我常会想起她，在这个物欲横流的残酷社会中她一路是怎样挣扎着走过的呢？损毁的容貌无论如何也无法使她变得魅力四射。我知道这对于她是个巨大的打击。

如果她外表美丽，她的生命能否会是另一番情形呢？或许会的。不过她有一种外表无法诠释的聪颖和秀美。她的声音正是我们所要聆听的那种，她的言语能轻易地进驻人们的心灵。她的隽语处于一颗受过伤害却满怀爱意的心，如所有人的心一样，只是她比别人更关注自己的心灵，更关注专心体会生活并从中学习获得提高。她有一种细腻的美。她生命中唯一惧怕的就是失去朋友。

如此高度的成熟我们要花费多长时间才可能达到呢？最终能否真正达到还不得而知。我们总是身心俱疲，怀才不遇，只担心眼前的不足，却忽视了那些经久不衰的东西。友谊珍贵且美好，要我们用心去呵护，有时简单的暗示便已足够了。比如偶尔给朋友写几句话，或把一些感人的美文写在纸条上投入篮子里，以供大家分享，让大家一起记住这美妙时刻的美好感觉。

她的生命真谛便是透过事物的表面认清其实质。她发现了美和慈爱，而美和慈爱也把她当作朋友，把生命的真谛展现给她。

心灵小语

"美丽"是怎样的定义呢？晶莹的双眸、坚挺的鼻梁、白皙的皮肤……这就是美丽吗？是不是有些贫乏呢？纯真、善良、坚强、聪慧……是不是更令人向往和崇敬呢？损毁的容颜也不能阻挡她对"美"的追求，以及对美好生活的向往。她是"美丽"的，因为她发现了"美"，并在"美"中展现其生命的真谛！

Beauty

Anonymous

There were a sensitivity and a beauty to her that have nothing to do with looks. She was one to be listened to, whose words were so easy to take to heart.

It is said that the true nature of being is veiled. The labor of words, the expression of art, the seemingly ceaseless buzz that is human thought all have in common the need to get at what really is so. The hope to draw close to and possess the truth of being can be a feverish one. In some cases it can even be fatal, if pleasure is one's truth and its attainment more important than life itself. In other lives, though, the search for what is truthful gives life.

I used to find notes left in the collection basket, beautiful notes about my homilies and about the writer's thoughts on the daily scriptural readings. The person who penned the notes would add reflections to my thoughts and would always include some quotes from poets and mystics he or she had read and remembered and loved. The notes fascinated me. Here was someone immersed in a search for truth and beauty. Words had been treasured, words that were beautiful. And I felt as if the words somehow delighted in being discovered, for they were obviously very generous to the as yet anonymous writer of the notes. And now this person was in turn learning the secret of sharing them. Beauty so shines when given away. The only truth that exists is, in that sense, free.

It was a long time before I met the author of the notes.

One Sunday morning, I was told that someone was waiting for me in the office. The young person who answered the rectory door said that it was "the woman who said she left all the notes." When I saw her I was shocked, since I immediately recognized her from church but had no idea that it was she who wrote the notes. She was sitting in a chair in the office with her hands folded in her lap. Her head was bowed and when she raised it to look at me, she could barely smile without pain. Her face was disfigured, and the skin so tight from surgical procedures that smiling or laughing was very difficult for her. She had suffered terribly from treatment to remove the growths that had so marred her face.

We chatted for a while that Sunday morning and agreed to meet for lunch later that week.

As it turned out we went to lunch several times, and she always wore a hat during the meal. I think that treatments of some sort had caused a lot of her hair to fall out. We shared things about our lives. I told her about my schooling and growing up. She told me that she had worked for years for an insurance company. She never mentioned family, and I did not ask.

We spoke of authors we both had read, and it was easy to tell that books are a great love of hers.

I have thought about her often over the years and how she struggled in a society that places an incredible premium on looks, class, wealth and all the other fineries of life. She suffered from a disfigurement that cannot be made to look attractive. I know that her condition hurt her deeply.

Would her life have been different had she been pretty? Chances are it would have. And yet there were a sensitivity and a beauty to her that had nothing to do with looks. She was one to be listened to, whose words were so easy to take to heart. Her words came from a wounded but loving heart, very much like all hearts, but she had more of a need to be aware of it, to live with it and learn from it. She possessed a fine-tuned sense of beauty. Her only fear in life was the loss of a friend.

How long does it take most of us to reach that level of human growth, if we ever get there? We get so consumed and diminished, worrying about all the things that need improving, we can easily forget to cherish those things that last. Friendship, so rare and so good, just needs our care—maybe even the simple gesture of writing a little note now and then, or the dropping of some beautiful words in a basket, in the hope that such beauty will be shared and taken to heart.

The truth of her life was a desire to see beyond the surface for a glimpse of what it is that matters. She found beauty and grace and they befriended her, and showed her what is real.

做你自己

佚名

小时候，我最喜欢在爷爷的农场里度过每一个星期天的下午，爷爷家在宾夕法尼亚州的西部。农场四周都围上了石墙，绵延数十里。房子和谷仓给我这个来自城市的男孩带来了无尽的乐趣。我早习惯了城里整洁如一的客厅，似乎在肃然警告："不许乱碰！"

记得我八岁那年，第一次去农场，就非常希望能爬农场周边的石墙。但我知道，父母是绝对不会同意的。这些墙年深日久，有些石头都不见了，还有些已经松动或崩溃。但是，我渴望爬这些墙的欲望如此强烈，终于在一个春天的下午，我鼓足勇气，走进客厅，大人们午餐后都会聚集在这里。

"我，呃，我想爬那些石墙，"我犹犹豫豫地说。大家都抬起头来。"我可以去爬那些石墙吗？"屋内的女士们立即异口同声地说道，"天啊，不可以！"她们惊慌地叫道，"你会伤着自己的！"我并不十分失望，这是我意料之中的结果。但就在我要离开客厅时，爷爷低沉的声音让我停了下来，"等一会儿，"我听见他说，"让孩子去爬石墙吧，他必须学会自己去做事。"

"快走吧，"他对我眨了眨眼，说道，"回来后找我。"接下来的两个半小时里，我爬这些古老的石墙，开心极了。后来，我把自己的历险告诉了爷爷。我永远也不会忘记他对我说的话，"弗雷德，"他笑着说，"你让这个日子非常特别，只是因为你做了一回自己。永远记住，整个世界只有一个你，我喜欢真实的你。"

许多年过去了，如今，我主持的电视节目《罗杰斯先生的街坊》，全美国有数以百万计的儿童在收看。随着时间的推移，节目发生了一些变化，但有一点始终没变——每期节目之后我都会传递给孩子这样一个信息，"这个世界只有一个你，"孩子们总会听我说，"人人都喜欢真实的你。"

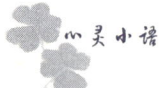

摆在我们面前的或许不仅仅只是一堵墙，也许是一座山、一片海，是勇敢地挑战自己，还是绕道而行，随波逐流呢？你是世上唯一的，要做最真实的自己！

Do Things for Himself

Anonymous

As a little boy, there was nothing I liked better than Sunday afternoons at my grandfather's farm in western Pennsylvania. Surrounded by miles of winding stonewalls, the house and barn provided endless hours of fun for a city kid like me. I was used to neat as a pin parlors that seemed to whisper, "Not to be touched!"

I can still remember one afternoon when I was eight years old. Since my first visit to the farm, I'd wanted more than anything to be allowed to climb the stonewalls surrounding the property. My parents would never approve. The walls were old; some stones were missing, others loose and crumbling. Still, my yearning to scramble across those walls grew so strong that finally, one spring afternoon, I summoned all my courage and entered the living room, where the adults had gathered after Sunday dinner.

"I, uh, I want to climb the stonewalls," I said hesitantly. Everyone looked up. "Can I climb the stone walls?" Instantly a chorus went up from the women in the room. "Heavens, no!" they cried in dismay, "You'll hurt yourself!" I wasn't too disappointed; the response was just as I'd expected. But before I could leave the room, I was stopped by my grandfather's booming voice. "Now hold on just a minute," I heard him say, "Let the boy climbs the stone walls. He has to learn to do things for himself."

"Scoot," he said to me with a wink, "and come and see me when you get back." For the next two and a half hours I climbed those old, walls and had the time of my life. Later I met with my grandfather to tell him about my adventure. I'll never forget what he said. "Fred," he said, grinning, "you made this day a special day just by being yourself. Always remember, there's only one person in this whole world like you, and I like you exactly as you are."

Many years have passed since then, and today I host the television program Mister Rogers' Neighborhood, seen by millions of children throughout America. There have been changes over the years, but one thing remains the same: my message to children at the end of almost every visit. "There's only one person in this whole world like you," the kids can count on hearing me say, "and people can like you exactly as you are."

论闲散

塞缪尔·约翰逊

很多德育家指出,骄傲是人类所有恶习中影响力最为广泛的。它的表现形式繁杂多样,隐藏方式也多种多样。就如同天边月儿晶莹透明的面纱,伪装既有光彩之处又有隐晦之所。虽然遮盖,亦可一眼望穿。

诚然,我无意降低骄傲的危害性程度,但不知道闲散是否会成为它的劲敌。

然而有些人高声赞叹闲散是高雅之事,以"闲散之士"自居,正如布西里斯在剧中自称为"骄傲之士"一样。他们炫耀自己无需做事,感谢命运之神没有给他们安排事情。他们每晚睡觉睡到自然醒,起床活动活动也只是为了更好地入睡。为了延长黑夜的主宰,他们拉起厚厚的双层窗帘,终日不见阳光,除了"告诉他,他们十分憎恶他的光芒"。不断地变换享受的姿势就是他们所有的劳动。对他们而言,昼夜的分别就在于长沙发、椅子和床的不同。

他们是一群真正的并且公开的闲散女神崇拜者。女神为其编织美丽的罂粟花环,把遗忘水倒入他们的杯中。他们生活在平静的愚蠢状态中,长久没有生命的气息。而死去时,生者只会说,他们停止了呼吸。

然而,不经意间,闲散主宰着多数人的生命。这种恶习仅限于散漫者自身,不会危及他人,因而就不同于欺诈和傲慢。前者危及财产安全;后者在他人的自卑中寻求满足。闲散是一种静默平和,既不会因他人之夸耀而心存妒忌,也不会因抗衡而产生敌意。正因为如此,他们不会惨遭责难。

就像傲慢时而藏于谦卑,闲散常掩于絮乱和匆忙。一个人疏于本职工作,自然就可能极力想些其他的事情,从而忘却自己曾经的蠢事;同时,他会把那些非职责范围内且需勤奋努力之事抛之脑后,这样他就能随心所欲,恣意而行了。

有些人时刻处于准备状态,致力于事前准备,拟计划,收集材料等。这些人必然受闲散女神某种神秘力量的控制。一味忙于找工具的工匠是无法有所成就的。一位绘画大师曾对我说,只对铅笔和色彩好奇之人,是不会精于绘画的。

也有另外一些人,他们把散漫看成权宜之计,认为生命会在闲散中碌碌而逝,而生活却不会在沉闷单调中了却。闲散之艺术就在于,用琐事填塞每一天,手头总有些让人好奇但不伤脑筋的事可做;同时,大脑保持在活动状态,而非劳动状态。

我的老朋友叟博就是一个闲散主义者,他的闲散艺术还卓有成效。他欲望强烈,思维敏锐,同时又热衷闲散,为在两者间寻求平衡,他很少难为自己。然而,欲望和思维的力量之强,令他无法安然入睡。即使如此,他也不会充分利用自身的特质,反倒愈对它们感到厌倦。

与人交谈是叟博的主要兴趣。他能无休止地交谈下去,并总能幻想自己是在教授或学习东西,远离了他人的指指点点,因而对他而言,讲话和聆听都是愉快的。

然而,有时候,为让朋友好好睡觉,他晚上必须回家;为不打扰他人,早上他得蹑手蹑脚。他一想到这些便会颤抖不已。不过他自有办法来缓解这些无聊时刻带来的痛苦。他常聊以自慰道,手工艺遭受了不应有的忽视。在很多方面,叟博发现了缜密思考,即推理的效应。周密的观察后,他开始购置工匠用具,并成功地修好了自家的煤箱。并且,一有机会,便继续做。

在其他时候,他还努力学习鞋匠、锡匠、管道工和陶工的技艺。尽管这些都没学成,他还是下定决心用知识武装自己,以胜任这些工艺。化学是他的日常消遣对象。他有个用于蒸馏的小炉子,长久以来,这就是他的抚慰品。他会在这个炉子上提取油、水、香精和烈酒。尽管他明白这些毫无用处,他还是坐下来,细数曲颈瓶里的水滴,忘却了——每滴的降落,意味着每一时刻的逝去。

可怜的叟博!我常用责备的口气取笑他,而他也常保证悔过自新。没人会如闲散者般承认错误,更没人真正拿出点行动。我不知道这篇文章会带来何种效应,或许叟博看后会付之一笑,然后继续烧炉子。但是,我很希望他能停下琐事,理智勤奋地做些有用之事。

作者在本文对"闲散"进行了全面、详细地诠释。不同的人对于"闲散"的看法也各有不同。有些人认为"闲散"是一件高雅之事,还以"闲散之士"自居,可是作者并不赞同,他认为"闲散"是一种恶习。还有一些人将"闲散"作为自己做事的驱动力,而另有一些人则把"闲散"作为生活的过渡。那"闲散"究竟意味着什么呢?仁者见仁,智者见智。 不过可以肯定的一点是——"闲散"并不是我们提倡的生活方式!

On Idleness

Samuel Johnson

Many moralists have remarked, that Pride has of all human vices the widest dominion, appears in the greatest **multiplicity**[1] of forms, and lies hid under the greatest variety of disguises; of disguises, which, like the moon's veil of brightness, are both its luster and its shade, and betray it to others, though they hide it from ourselves.

It is not my intention to degrade Pride from this **preeminence**[2] of mischief, yet I know not whether Idleness may not maintain a very doubtful and obstinate competition.

There are some that profess Idleness in its full dignity, who call themselves the Idle, as Busiris in the play "calls himself the Proud"; who boast that they do nothing, and thank their stars that they have nothing to do; who sleep every night till they can sleep no longer, and rise only that exercise may enable them to sleep again; who prolong the reign of darkness by double curtains, and never see the sun but to "tell him how they hate his beams"; whose whole labor is to vary the postures of **indulgence**[3], and whose day differs from their night but as a couch or chair differs from a bed.

These are the true and open votaries of Idleness, for whom she weaves the garlands of poppies, and into whose cup she pours the waters of oblivion; who exist in a state of unruffled stupidity, forgetting and forgotten; who have long ceased to live, and at whose death the survivors can only say, that they have ceased to breathe.

But Idleness predominates in many lives where it is not suspected; for being a vice which terminates in itself, it may be enjoyed without injury to others; and is therefore not watched like Fraud, which endangers property, or like Pride, which naturally seeks its gratifications in another's inferiority. Idleness is a silent and peaceful quality, that neither raises envy by ostentation, nor hatred by opposition; and therefore nobody is busy to censure or detect it.

As Pride sometimes is hid under humility, Idleness is often covered by **turbulence**[4] and hurry. He that neglects his known duty and real employment, naturally endeavors to crowd his mind with something that may bar out the remembrance of his own folly, and does anything but what he ought to do with eager diligence, that he may keep himself in his own favor.

Some are always in a state of preparation, occupied in previous measures, forming plans, accumulating materials, and providing for the main affair. These are certainly under the secret power of Idleness. Nothing is to be expected from the workman whose tools are forever to be sought. I was once told by a great master, that no man ever excelled in painting, who was eminently curious about pencils and colors.

There are others to whom Idleness dictates another expedient, by which life may be passed unprofitably away without the **tediousness**[5] of many vacant hours. The art is, to fill the day with petty business, to have always something in hand which may raise curiosity, but not solicitude, and keep the mind in a state of action, but not of labor.

This art has for many years been practiced by my old friend Sober, with wonderful success. Sober is a man of strong desires and quick imagination, so exactly balanced by the love of ease, that they can seldom stimulate him to any difficult undertaking; they have, however, so much power, that they will not suffer him to lie quite at rest, and though they do not make him sufficiently useful to others, they make him at least weary of himself.

Mr.Sober's chief pleasure is conversation; there is no end of his talk or his attention; to speak or to hear is equally pleasing; for he still fancies that he is teaching or learning something, and is free for the time from his own reproaches.

But there is one time at night when he must go home, that his friends may sleep; and another time in the morning, when all the world agrees to shut out interruption. These are the moments of which poor Sober trembles at the thought. But the misery of these tiresome intervals, he has many means of alleviating. He has persuaded himself that the manual arts are undeservedly overlooked; he has observed in many trades the effects of close thought, and just **ratiocination**[6]. From speculation he proceeded to practice, and supplied himself with the tools of a carpenter, with which he mended his coalbox very successfully, and which he still continues to employ, as he finds occasion.

He has attempted at other times the crafts of the shoemaker, tinman, plumber, and potter; in all these arts he has failed, and resolves to qualify himself for them by better information. But his daily amusement is chemistry. He has a small furnace, which he employs in distillation, and which has long been the solace of his life. He draws oils and waters, and essences and spirits, which he knows to be of no use; sits and counts the drops as they come from his retort, and forgets that, whilst a drop is falling, a moment flies away.

Poor Sober! I have often teased him with reproof, and he has often promised reformation; for no man is so much open to conviction as the Idler, but there is none on whom it operates so little. What will be the effect of this paper I know not; perhaps he will read it and laugh, and light the fire in his furnace; but my hope is that he will quit his trifles, and betake himself to rational and useful diligence.

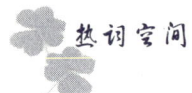
热词空间

1. multiplicity [ˌmʌltiˈplisiti] *n.* 多样性
2. preeminence [pri(ː)ˈeminəns] *n.* 卓越
3. indulgence [inˈdʌldʒ(ə)ns] *v.* 放任
4. turbulence [ˈtəːbjuləns] *n.* 骚乱；动荡
5. tediousness [ˈtiːdiəsnis] *n.* 沉闷
6. ratiocination [ˌrætiɔsiˈneiʃən] *n.* 推理；推论

过平静生活的代价是什么

佚名

我们渴望生活在一个安宁的时代,宁静的社区,和睦的家庭。当问起人们他们最想得到的东西时,调查表明,"宁静的心态"居于首位。尽管如此,就像许多我们想要的事物一样,需要进行交易。你准备好支付了吗?

如果你仍然与前面的驾驶员争论不休,你就不会拥有平静。如果你坚信你的做事方式是唯一的,你就不会拥有平静。如果你指责别人胜过自我反省,你就不会拥有平静。平静是人们创造出来的。它是人们以更好的方式相处的共识,也是一种义务。那就是……平静。

你的性情是怎样的呢?你时常给别人提供意见吗?

哦,你甚至不用开口去评断。只要转移视线就行。留给你想象的空间并不多。

记住,你必须要与人沟通。平静是交易的纽带。每个人都必须付帐或者他们不能运用自如。对于平静,这里有几个方法需要记住:

首先致力于自我发展

当你发现你在评价别人时,首先问问你自己是否有这个资格。当你很负责地下定结论时,你最好想想是否对他人有帮助。

致力于解决问题,而不是问题本身。

不要寻找别人的过错,要将精力集中于去创造一个调整状况或是避免错误再次发生的方法上。

正确判断自己的感觉

用点时间来正确判断你当时的感觉,并赋予它一个名字。人们在描述的过程中都会明白其中的恐惧、挫败和痛苦。谈论的过程会有助于交流。恼怒是你内心燃起的对于恐惧、挫败或是痛苦的反应。

有责任心,可靠,适度

尊重自己和他人许下的诺言。怀疑时,行动要比语言更有力。言行不一致时,要相信行为。并且,言行一致。

凡事保持平衡

你有资格拥有自己的看法、信仰、价值观和生活方式。你的选择是你和他人的判断。

在表达和行事之前要考虑后果。要拥有平静,不要侵犯他人的权益以及他人拥有自己的看法、信仰、价值观和生活方式的自由。平静的生活要求宽容、接受以及良好的自我防护。

清楚地了解,对你来说什么才是重要的,有意义和有价值的

当你在了解自己的价值观并基于其生活时,你就会找到平静。随后,与他人分享。你不会赠与他人你没有的礼物。

当你以这些方式行事时,你就会拥有平静的代价。这是唯一获取的方法,如果你想要保留它,你必须要付出代价!

平静的生活是每个人都向往的,可是不论做什么事,都是需要付出的,平静的生活也不例外。本文对如何使自己处于平静作出了详细的介绍,想必大家在阅读之后心里都有了各自的想法。其实只要自己心平气和的与人相处,达到这个愿望就易如反掌了。

What Is the Price of Personal Peace

Anonymous

We want to live in peaceful times, in peaceful communities, in peaceful families. When asked what people wanted most in their lives, surveys showed that peace of mind topped the list. As with most things we want, though, it has a price. Are you prepared to pay?

If you are still yelling at the driver in front of you, there cannot be peace. If you believe your way is the only way, there cannot be peace. If you are more likely to judge others than reflect on yourself, there cannot be peace. Peace is a construct of people. It is an agreement that there is a better way to live, and a **commitment**[1] to that way. That way is... peacefully.

How's your temper? Do you offer others a piece of your mind often?

Oh, you do not even have to open your mouth to pass judgment. Just roll or **avert**[2] your eyes. That doesn't leave too much to the imagination.

Remember, you cannot not communicate. Peace has a price tag. Each person has to pay it or they simply cannot have it. Here are a few ways to save up for it:

Work on Your Self-development First

When you find yourself judging others, first ask yourself if you are blameless in those areas. When you have taken care of the issue responsibly yourself, you will better understand how to be most helpful to others.

Focus on Solutions not Problems

Rather than looking for someone to blame, put your energy into creating a better way to rectify a situation or to prevent a **recurrence**[3] Work towards agreement for solutions. That's a much better use for your energy.

Identify Your Feelings Correctly

Take the time to identify the feeling you are experiencing accurately and give it a name. People can understand fear, frustration and pain when it is described. Talking about it brings clarity to communication. Anger is an arousal in your body in response to fear, frustration or pain. Simply being angry causes folks to move away from you.

Be Accountable, Responsible and Congruent

Keep your commitments to yourself and others. When in doubt, actions speak louder than words. When behavior is not congruent with words, believe the behavior. And, walk your talk.

Maintain Your Balance

You are entitled to your opinions, beliefs, values and lifestyle. Your choices have consequences for you and others.

Consider the consequences before acting or speaking. To have peace, it is essential to live without infringing on the rights and freedoms of others to have their opinions, beliefs, values and lifestyle. Peaceful living requires tolerance, acceptance, and, good fences and boundaries.

Be Very Clear about What Is Important, Significant and Valuable to You

When you know what you value and live accordingly, you will find peace. Then, it is yours to share. You cannot give a gift you do not have.

When you have conserved your energy in these ways, you will have the price of peace. There is only one catch. If you want to keep it, you simply have to keep paying the price!

热词空间

1. commitment [kəˈmitmənt] n. 委托事项;许诺;承担义务
2. avert [əˈvəːt] v. 转移
3. recurrence [riˈkʌrəns] n. 复发;重;循环

充满活力愉快地生活

佚名

充满活力、愉快地生活……问问自己下面的问题,按照你所知道的,并且能够实现你所需要的不同行事。简单吗?当然!容易吗?不一定!它能做出既巨大又奇妙的改变吗?你可以相信。

做哪些事情可以帮助你处于最佳状态,你可以与世界协调起来,充满爱心、自信、慷慨和耐性。成为勇猛、敏感、开放、友爱和忠心之人。然后系统地摆脱分心、耗力、烦忧、渴望或任何一种类型的难题。明确的判断自己(它们会不知不觉地走近我们,我们就去适应它们)——问问你自己下面这些问题。

我设定怎样的目标,才能使我:

能够充满活力愉快地生活?

不会筋疲力尽?

不会焦虑或担忧?

不会烦躁不安?

不会因某种环境或人类的影响而变得消极?

你能做到活力四射、精神充沛、开心快乐地生活吗?其实答案就是自信、勇敢、宽容、热情地生活,不要忧愁满腹、怨声载道,要对一切都充满希望。这些听起来很简单,可是做起来就不那么容易了。问问自己,能做到吗?

To Be Full of Energy, Joy and Life

Anonymous

To be full of energy, joy and life... ask yourself such questions as these, and take what actions you know will make the difference you need. Simple? You bet! Easy? Not necessarily! Will it make a huge and wonderful difference? You can be sure of it.

Do those things that help you be your best self, **attuned with**[1] the universe, loving, confident, generous, and patient. Being bold, **vulnerable**[2], open, loving, and committed. Then systematically get rid of **distractions**[3], drains, causes of worry, anxiety or problems of any kind. To identify these clearly for yourself (they tend to sneak up on us and we tend to get used to them)—ask yourself questions such as these.

What limits do I set, so that:

So I can be being full of energy, joy and life?

I am not being drained of energy?

I do not worry or be anxious?

I am not distracted?

I am not negatively affected by certain circumstances or people?

1. attune with 与……协调
2. vulnerable ['vʌlnərəbl] *adj.* 易受伤害的
3. distraction [dis'trækʃən] *n.* 分心; 分心的事情

美丽英文
Beautiful English

阴郁的日子

佚名

人人都有烦恼的日子。在这样的日子里,我们满怀仇怨、脾气暴躁、寂寞难耐、精神委靡,也会自惭形秽、自怨自艾,甚至乱作一团。于是我们就很难重振旗鼓,开始新生活。郁闷的日子里,我们可能变得偏执,认为自己成了所有人的攻击对象(事实上,情况一般不是这样);我们会感到异常失望或万分焦虑,甚至会神经质地咬指甲,疯狂地吞下三大块巧克力蛋糕!痛苦的日子里,我们沉浸于悲伤的海洋,随时都会不知缘由地泪流满面。最终,我们就会觉得活着毫无意义,不知道还能坚持多久,有时就想大吼,"来,给我一枪吧!"其实就那么一点小事,足足可以让我们郁闷一天。也许,我们忽略了自身的优点,倒是发现额头平添了几条皱纹,体重增加了几斤,或鼻子上多长了粉刺;也许,约会对象的名字也忘了,那张滑稽的照片也登出来了;也许,被人抛弃、离婚、被老板解雇,当众出丑,被难听的绰号折磨得身心憔悴,或是因那天的发型糟糕透顶;也许,因不堪工作之苦,成为别人的笑柄;也许,身肩重任,老板却百般刁难,同事苦苦相讥;也许,我们头疼欲裂、口臭,牙疼,吹牛皮,唇干舌燥,指甲长到肉里。不论什么原因,我们都认为,有人厌恶着我们。哦,怎么办呢,怎么办?

也许,像大多数人一样,我们会认为事情自有解决之道。结果呢,后半辈子我们都在回望昨日,期待着往事重演。最后呢,我们变得狂暴,愤世嫉俗,令人同情。最终深感绝望,于是乞求上帝收回我们的生命,或是整日沉浸在比利·乔的蓝调音乐中。这种心态岂不疯狂?要知道,年轻只有一次,年老也如此。我们又将有什么奇遇,谁能预料到呢?

毕竟,这是个充满惊奇的世界,未来是无法预知的。这里,我们可以分享美味可口的小吃;可能会拥有难以数计的财富,甚至可能成为天王巨星。这似乎很好啊,不是吗?还有很多呢!我们还可以玩倒立,游戏,练瑜伽,唱卡拉OK,跳充满激情和野性的热舞,但最好的莫过于与爱人罗曼蒂克了。那意味着久久梦幻般地凝视对方,在耳边私语,拥抱,热吻。怎样才能找到那种幸福的感觉——"就像滑入充满激情的泡泡浴里的感觉?"其实很简单。

　　首先,不要逃避那些困扰我们的问题,要敢于面对。放松一下,听听音乐,深呼吸。如果可能,试着沉思冥想,或者散散步,清醒一下大脑。放下情感包袱,接受既成事实。换位思考问题,或许,症结就在自身。如果真的是这样,大气地说声对不起(这样做,永远不会为时已晚);如果是别人错了,站出来,勇敢地说句,"不对,我认为不是那样的!"语气硬点,没关系(也可以适时发出嘘声)。可以为自己骄傲,但不要忘记自嘲一下(和乐观的人交往容易的多)。过好每一天,想象生命在今天就要终结,因为那天终将来到。对于那些力所能及以外之事,不要怯于尝试,要敢于冒风险;不要踌躇不前,走出去,大胆去做。毕竟,生命的意义就在于此。

　　我也是这样认为的。

　　人人都有烦恼,阴郁的日子随时都会降临,每当这个时候,你会怎样应对呢?或许你会心情消极,任由烦恼的病毒侵入全身,最终崩溃。可是这样你甘心吗?这样的你未免太懦弱了,当困难到来时,我们要勇敢地与之搏斗,要以智取胜。本文就为大家介绍了许多解除忧愁的好方法,想必会使大家摆脱困境,受益匪浅!

The Blue Day

Anonymous

Everybody has blue days. These are miserable days when you feel **lousy**[1], grumpy, lonely and utterly exhausted. Days when you feel small and insignificant, when everything seems just out of reach. You can't rise to the occasion. Just getting started seems impossible. On blue days you can become paranoid that everyone is out to get you. (This is not always such a bad thing.) You feel frustrated and anxious, which can induce a nail-biting frenzy that can escalate into a triple-chocolate-mud-cake-eating frenzy in a blink of an eye! On blue days you feel like you're floating in an ocean of sadness. You're about to burst into tears at any moment and you don't even know why. Ultimately, you feel like you are wandering through life without purpose. You're not sure how much longer you can hang on and you feel like shouting, "Will someone please shoot me!" It doesn't take much to bring on a blue day. You might just wake up not feeling or looking your best, find some new wrinkles, put on a little weight, or get a huge pimple on your nose. You could forget your date's name or have an embarrassing photograph published. You might get dumped, divorced, or fired, make fool of yourself in public, be afflicted with a demeaning nickname, or just have a plain old bad-hair day. Maybe work is a pain in the **butt**[2] You're under major pressure to fill someone else's shoes, your boss is picking on you, and everyone in the office is driving you crazy. You might have a splitting headache, or a slipped disk, bad breath, a toothache, chronic gas, dry lips, or an ingrown toenail. Whatever the reason, you're convinced that someone up there doesn't like you. Oh what to do, what to do?

Well, if you're like most people, you'll hide behind a flimsy belief that everything will sort itself out. Then you will spend the rest of your life looking over your shoulder, waiting for everything to go wrong all over again. All the while becoming crusty and cynical or a pathetic, sniveling victim. Until you get so depressed that you lie down and beg the earth to swallow you up or, even worse, become addicted to Billy Joel songs. This is crazy, because you're only young once and you're never old twice. Who knows what fantastic things are in store just around the corner?

After all, the world is full of amazing discoveries, things you can't even imagine now. There are delicious, happy sniffs and scrumptious snacks to share. Hey, you might end up fabulously rich or even become a huge superstar (one day). Sounds good, doesn't it? But wait, there's more! There are handstands, and games to play and yoga and karaoke and wild, crazy, bohemian dancing. But best of all, there's romance. Which means long dreamy stares, whispering sweet nothings, cuddles, smooches, more smooches and even more smooches, a frisky love bite or two, and then, well, anything goes. So how can you find that blissful "just sliding into a hot bubble bath" kind of feeling? It's easy.

First, stop slinking away from all those nagging issues. It's time to face the music. Now just relax. Take some deep breaths (in through the nose and out through the mouth). Try to meditate if you can. Or go for a walk to clear your head. Accept the fact that you'll have to let go of some emotional baggage. Try seeing things from a different perspective. Maybe you're actually the one at fault. If that's the case, be big enough to say you're sorry (it is never too late to do this). If someone else is doing the wrong thing, stand up and say, "That's not right and I won't stand for it!" It's OK to be forceful. (It's really okay to blow **raspberries**[3.]) Be proud of who you are, but don't lose the ability to laugh at yourself. (This is a lot easier when you associate with positive people). Live every day as gift were your last, because one day it will be. Don't be afraid to bite off more than you can chew. Take big risks. Never hang back. Get out there and go for it. After all, isn't that what life is all about?

I think so too.

热词空间

1. lousy ['lauzi] *adj.* 糟糕的
2. butt [bʌt] *n.* 笑柄
3. raspberry ['ræzberi] *n.* [俚]罪（表示憎恶；嘲笑；不赞成）咂舌声

美丽英文
Beautiful English

感触美丽

佚名

有时,我会问朋友(非盲人)的所见所闻。最近,一位与我很要好的朋友来看我。她刚从树林散步回来。于是,我问她在树林里都看见了什么。她说:"没看到什么特别的。"我很早就相信:有眼睛的人往往看不到什么东西,要不是早习惯了这样的回答,我或许会感到很吃惊。

我问自己,这怎么可能呢? 在树林里走了那么长时间,没看到什么东西? 我,一个盲人,仅通过触觉就可以发现很多有趣的东西。我能感觉到一片树叶的均匀对称;用手轻轻划过白桦树或松树时,能感觉到白桦树光滑和松树粗糙的表皮。春天,我触摸树枝,满怀希望地寻找新芽,那是大自然经过一个冬天的沉睡后苏醒的第一个标志。我能感觉到有着天鹅绒般肌理的可爱花朵,发现它层层地绽放着。于是,大自然的神奇展现在我面前。有时候,我会将手轻轻地放在一棵小树上,幸运的话,还能感觉到高歌的小鸟快乐地颤动。当我把手伸进小溪,那冰凉的水从指缝流过时,我欣喜万分。对我而言,一张青绿的松针毯或一片柔软的青草地比那最为奢华的波斯地毯更令人赏心悦目;四季的交替是一场激动人心且永不落幕的戏剧演出,出演的每一个动作都划过我的指尖。内心不时地呼喊着,我多想亲眼看看这一切啊! 仅通过触觉,我就能获得如此多的快乐,如果我能看见的话,那将会有多少美丽的事物呈现在我眼前啊! 然而,看得见的人却看不到什么,这个色彩斑斓、生机盎然的世界在他们眼中是那么平淡无奇。也许,这就是人类——不珍惜已经拥有的,却渴望没有拥有的。在这个光明的世界里,视力仅被当作一种便利而不是丰富生活的工具,这是怎样的一种遗憾啊!

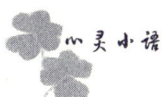

视力健全的人们可能不会想到要驻足欣赏一下周围的美景,享受这五光十色的世界。可是对于那些双明失明的人来说,美丽的花儿、高歌的小鸟、青绿的松柏……是多么奢侈的一件事啊! 可是他们并没有因此而放弃感受美丽的可能……

Feeling Beauty

Anonymous

Now and then I have tested my seeing friends to discover what they see. Recently I was visited by a very good friend who had just returned from a long walk in the woods, and I asked her what she had observed. "Nothing in particular," she replied. I might have been incredulous had I not been accustomed to such responses, for long ago I became convinced that the seeing see little.

How was it possible, I asked myself, to walk for an hour through the woods and see nothing worthy of note? I who cannot see find hundreds of things to interest me through mere touch. I feel the delicate symmetry of a leaf. I pass my hands lovingly about the smooth skin of a silver birch, or the rough shaggy bark of a pine. In spring I touch the branches of trees hopefully in search of a bud, the first sign of awakening Nature after her winter's sleep. I feel the delightful, velvety texture of a flower, and discover its remarkable convolutions; and something of the miracle of Nature is revealed to me. Occasionally, if I am very fortunate, I place my hand gently in a small tree and feel the happy quiver of a bird in full song. I am delighted to have cool waters of a brook rush through my open fingers. To me a lush carpet of pine needles or spongy grass is more welcome than the most luxurious Persian rug. To me the pageant of seasons is a thrilling and unending drama, the action of which streams through my finger tips. At times my heart cries out with longing to see all these things. If I can get so much pleasure from mere touch, how much more beauty must be revealed by sight. Yet, those who have eyes apparently see little. The panorama of color and action filling the world is taken for granted. It is human, perhaps, to appreciate little that which we have and to long for that which we have not, but it is a great pity that in the world of light and the gift of sight is used only as mere convenience rather than as a means of adding fullness to life.

美丽英文
Beautiful English

喜悦的能力

查理·爱德华·蒙太古

在心智的各种能力中,有一种能力对于许多儿童和艺术家来说是与生俱来的,而且一旦获得它,就终身不会失去。这种能力就是对一件事物,甚至对每件事物都感到喜悦的能力。之所以感到喜悦,并不是因为那件事物是达到其他目的的手段,只是因为这件事情本身,正如一个情人觉得他所喜爱的对象是十全十美一样。一个心智健康的儿童也许会把他的手放在夏天的草地上,抚摸着它,他觉得坚实的大地也有点弹性,因而打心眼里感到欣喜。他并不会考虑这草地对于人们玩游戏或用来放羊会有多大好处。如果这样的话,那就是一心贪图钱财的追求者的恶劣行径了。但这孩子内心的喜悦却是至真至纯的,是对这件事物的内在特性感到真正的心醉神迷。不管这些事物是什么,也不管它们对什么有用或者没用,它们自然地存在着,有着自己动人的外观与感觉,就像一张面孔那样;油漆下面冰凉的钢铁,温暖可亲的彩色木料,拿在手中一揉就碎的令人着迷的土块,微微含着日晒与荨麻的干燥气味;各种普通的事物都有着可爱的差别,因而都突显了其独特的性格。

初到伊甸园的亚当左右张望,充满喜悦,这正是一个正常的儿童在做什么或看什么时所感到的欣喜之情。如果让他拿起人们使用的真正的铲子去做点普通的劳动,那他肯定会感到一种神秘的喜悦。当他经过一番辛劳,帮助园丁把花园里的杂草除掉,两只脚像缩进身体里似的走了回来(像法国人说的那样),他会在一片纯粹的喜悦之光的照耀下安然睡去……

看到这篇文章的题目,你一定会疑惑,难道喜悦也要有能力才可以做到吗?喜悦对于每个人来说意义都是不同的,对于小孩子来说,喜悦是发自内心的,是干干脆脆的,而对于那些一味金钱至上的人们来说,喜悦只是他们劣行的帮凶。

The Faculty of Delight

Charles Edward Montague

Among the mind's powers is one that comes of itself to many children and artists. It need not be lost, to the end of his days, by any one who has ever had it. This is the power of taking delight in a thing, or rather in anything, everything, not as a means to some other end, but just because it is what it is, as the lover dotes on whatever may be the traits of the beloved object. A child in the full health of his mind will put his hand flat on the summer turf, feel it, and give a little shiver of private glee at the **elastic**[1] firmness of the globe. He is not thinking how well it will do for some game or to feed sheep upon. That would be the way of the wooer whose mind runs on his mistress's money. The child's is sheer affection, the true **ecstatic**[2] sense of the thing's inherent characteristics. No matter what the things may be, no matter what they are good or no good for, there they are, each with a thrilling unique look and feel of its own, like a face; the iron astringently coop under its paint, the painted wood familiarly warmer, the clod crumbling enchantingly down in the hands, with its little dry smell of the sun and of hot nettles; each common thing a personality marked by delicious differences.

The joy of an Adam new to the garden and just looking round is brought by the normal child to the things that he does as well as those that he sees. To be suffered to do some plain work with the real spade used by mankind can give him a mystical exaltation: to come home with his legs, as the French say, reentering his body from the fatigue of helping the gardener to weed beds sends him to sleep in the glow of a beatitude that is an end in itself...

热词空间

1. elastic [i'læstik] *adj.* 弹性的
2. ecstatic [eks'tætik] *adj.* 狂喜的；心醉神迷的；入迷的

我喜欢这种淡淡的感觉

佚名

我喜欢枝头上淡绿的嫩芽——它是春天的使者,是一天中清晨的开始……
我喜欢天空中淡淡的浮云,它使天空显得更为广阔、蔚蓝和无边无际……

我喜欢淡淡的风。春天,微风亲吻脸颊;秋天,微风温柔抚面;夏日,微风送来凉爽;冬日,微风吹来寒意……

我喜欢品淡淡的茶,只一小口,就醇香绕齿。淡淡的苦才是它的原味……

我喜欢淡淡的友谊。彼此不必天天在一起,偶尔一句问候就能让思念蔓延……

我喜欢淡淡地想念朋友,独自倚在沙发上,任思绪在回忆中飘荡……

爱情也可以是淡淡的。这样,才不至成为爱情的囚徒,为爱情所缚;就是那样,不多、不少,只是淡淡的……

淡淡的友情很诚;淡淡的问候很醇;淡淡的情爱很柔;淡淡的思念很深;淡淡的祝福很真……

忙于工作、勤于家庭的朋友们,在你们忙碌之余是否想到要去享受一下户外淡绿的嫩芽、淡淡的浮云、淡淡的风、淡淡的茶……来去匆匆不是我们生活的追求,享受生活才是我们的真正目标。这种淡淡的感觉会给我们忙碌的生活增添一抹阳光,让我们在这淡淡的感觉中体味纯净的美丽!

I Like the Subtle Feeling

Anonymous

I like the subtle fresh green budding from the branches of the tree—the **herald**[1] of spring, ushering in the dawn...

I like the subtle flow of cloud that makes the sky seem even more vast, **azure**[2] and immense...

I like the subtle wind. In spring, it steals a kiss on my cheek; in autumn, it caresses my face; in summer, it brings in cool sweet smell; in winter, it carries a crisp chilliness...

I like the subtle taste of tea that last long after a sip. The subtle bitter is what it is meant to be...

I like the subtle friendship that does not hold people together. Instead, an occasional greeting spreads our longings far beyond...

I like the subtle longing for a friend, when I sink deeply in a couch, mind wandering in memories of the past...

Love should also be subtle, without **enslaving**[3] the ones fallen into her arms. Not a bit less nor a bit more...

Subtle friendship is true; subtle greetings are enough; subtle love is tender; subtle longing is deep; subtle wishes come from the bottom of your heart...

1. herald ['herəld] *n.* 使者;先驱;预兆
2. azure ['æʒə] *n.* 天蓝色;苍天;碧空
3. enslave [in'sleiv] *v.* 奴役;束缚;沉溺

飘逸而行

佚名

人在旅途，难免有不安与困惑伴你同行，但不管怎样，你都要继续自己的人生之旅。人生之旅的目的因人而异。有的人步履匆忙，心急意切，他们只关注最终目标，却根本无暇观赏路边的风景。可路途漫漫，终点何在呢？有的人像游客，不紧不慢，时而停下来观花开花落，看云卷云舒，时而逆风而行，冒雨而进，他们不会苦恼，因为敞开的心网，已将烦躁与苦恼过滤。

狭促的工作场所，拥挤的居住空间，局限的社交圈子——人们对这一成不变的单调越来越不满。然而，如果一个人随遇而安，总能找到安宁与舒适。浩淼的大千世界，一个人只能占据其中微小的一隅。然而，比海洋更大的是天空，比天空更大的是人的心灵，因为有一对想象的翅膀进驻于这小小的心灵，它可以尽情地飞翔。

只有当一个人发觉自己失去了许许多多时，最终才会赢得他想要的东西，或许他会得不偿失。

人生旅途上，一些人带着疲乏的追名逐利之心奋力前行，另一些人却自在逍遥地与自然和谐相处，飘逸而行。

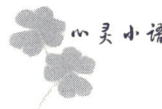

在这个世界上，不同的人，有不同的生活方式，有的人追逐名利，忘乎所以；有的人来去匆匆，繁事缠身；有的人不紧不慢，享受生活。哪一种才是我们想要的生活呢？当我们为了一些自以为很重要的事，而放弃了某些其实很重要的事，到头来却发现，生活，还是要飘逸而行！

Go Easy and Enjoy Yourself in Harmony

Anonymous

To go on a journey is often worrisome, but so long as one lives he proceeds on his life's journey. Different people go along differently. Some take hasty steps in anxiety. Obsessed with reaching the next goal in time, they spare no time for sight-seeing along the way, nor do they have a clear view where their long roads end. Others travel leisurely like tourists. They would take time off now and then for a look at blooming flowers or fallen petals. They would stop to admire clouds gathering and dispersing. Even when they go against the wind or are caught in the rain, they never get annoyed, for worries slip off their minds as if from an open net.

Cramped is one's workplace. Narrow is one's residence and small is the social circle one moves about—such limitedness in space entail lack of variety which is the source of some people's complaint. But a person is always able to find peace and comfort if he takes things as they are. Compared with the vastness of the universe it is only a tiny spot one occupies on earth. However, though larger than the ocean is the sky, even larger is the human mind, for in it imagination would come and go on the wing without limitations.

One may eventually win what he has set his mind to, only to find that he has lost quite a lot. Perhaps what he loses is even better than what he gains.

On one's journey of life some people hurry on with a heavy heart in pursuit of fame and wealth while others go easy and enjoy themselves in harmony with nature.

美丽英文
Beautiful English

就为了今天

佚名

就为了今天，我将努力只为度过今天，而不是立刻去解决终生问题。我可以花12个小时去做某件事，但如果我觉得要持续一生去做的话，我一定会心惊胆战。

就为了今天，我要快乐。亚伯拉罕·林肯说得很对："大多数人之所以快乐，是因为他们决定要这样。"

就为了今天，我要调整自己适应一切，而不是让每一件事都合乎我的心愿。好运降临时，我会好好把握。

就为了今天，我会充实我的头脑。我要学习，学习一些实用的，不做精神的流浪者。

就为了今天，我会用三种方法磨炼我的灵魂。我要做一件对某人有利的事，但不能被发现。如果有人发现了，那就不算。我至少要做两件不想做的事——只是为了磨炼。我受伤的心绪不会向任何人袒露，也许的确是伤痛，但我不会表现出来。

就为了今天，我要做一个使人愉快的人。我要尽可能地看起来令人满意。我要打扮得体，言谈温和、举止亲切、不言是非，努力改善自身，而不是管制他人。

就为了今天，我要有一个安排。可能我不会严格遵循，但有了安排，就可以避免两种弊端：仓促行事和优柔寡断。

就为了今天，我要独处宁静的半个小时，放松身心。在这半个小时里，我会在某个时刻试着去更好地感悟人生。

就为了今天，我无所畏惧。特别是，我不再害怕享受美好。我要相信，我对世界付出多少，世界也会回报多少。

今天的意义不同于昨天、明天，它的意义在于享受现在，我们不用高喊明天我们要比昨天怎样怎样，只要对自己说，我今天很开心，很幸福，过得很充实。

Just for Today

Anonymous

Just for today I will try to live through this day only and not tackle my whole life problem at once. I can do something for twelve hours that would appall me if I felt that I had to keep it up for a lifetime.

Just for today I will be happy. This assumes to be true what Abraham Lincoln said, that "Most folks are as happy as they make up their minds to be."

Just for today I will adjust myself to what is, and not try to adjust everything to my own desires. I will take my "luck" as it comes.

Just for today I will try to strengthen my mind. I will study. I will learn something useful. I will not be a mental loafer.

Just for today I will exercise my soul in three ways. I will do somebody a good turn and not get found out: if anybody knows of it, it will not count. I will do at least two things I don't want to do—just for exercise. I will not show anyone that my feelings are hurt: they may be hurt, but today I will not show it.

Just for today I will be agreeable. I will look as well as I can, dress becomingly, talk low, act courteously, criticize not one bit, and try not to improve or regulate anybody but myself.

Just for today I will have a program. I may not follow it exactly, but I will have it. I will save myself from two pests: hurry and indecision.

Just for today I will have a quiet half hour all by myself and relax. During this half hour, sometime, I will try to get a better perspective of my life.

Just for today I will be unafraid. Especially I will not be afraid to enjoy what is beautiful, and to believe that as I give to the world, so the world will give to me.

想想你所拥有的

佚名

　　专注于我们想得到的,而不是我们所拥有的,这是我见过的一种最具普遍性和破坏性的心理趋向。我们拥有多少,似乎并无太大区别,我们欲望的清单不断扩充,使我们永远不满足。"当我实现了这个愿望,就会快乐。"一旦这个欲望得到满足,以后还会出现相同的欲求心理。

　　我们想要这个或那个。如果得不到,就会不断地去想那些没有的东西,总是感到不满足。而如果得到了,在新的条件下,我们又产生同样的心理。所以,尽管我们得到了,还是不开心。如果我们一味地渴求新的欲望,将无法找到幸福。

　　幸运的是,我们想要获得幸福,有这样一种方法:转换我们思考的重心,从想要的转移到拥有的。我们可以试着去想伴侣的可贵品质,而不去希求她该如何与现在不同;可以为自己拥有一份工作充满感激,而不去抱怨薪水太低;可以设想闭门在家的种种乐趣,而不是渴望去夏威夷度假。可以这样去考虑的事物无穷无尽!一旦你意识到自己又陷入这个思维陷阱:"我希望生活不是这样"时,要退后一步,重新思考,深呼吸,想想你所拥有的。这样,感激之情便会油然而生。当你关注的不再是自己想要的,而是所拥有的时,你最终得到的一定会比想要的更多;如果你关注伴侣的优秀品德,她就会更可爱;如果你对工作充满感激,而不是抱怨,你会做得更好,工作效率会更高,薪水也可能提高;如果你在家能自得其乐,而不是等着去夏威夷享受,你会找到更多的乐趣。假设你真的去了夏威夷,往往会更快乐,即使因为某种偶然没能去成,仍然会过得开心。

　　记住,从现在开始,多想想你拥有的,而不是你想要的。如果你这样做,你的生活就会比以前更美好,那种感受或许将是你生命中第一次,你将会懂得心满意足的含义。

　　多想想你拥有的,而不是你想要的。这样你的心情也会轻松许多。懂得享受现在的人才是最幸福的人,也是最懂得生活真谛的人。

Think More about What You Have

Anonymous

One of the most pervasive and destructive mental tendencies I've seen is that of focusing on what we want instead of what we have. It doesn't seem to make any difference how much we have; we just keep expanding our list of desires, which guarantees we will remain dissatisfied. The mind-set that says "I'll be happy when this desire is fulfilled" is the same mind-set that will repeat itself once that desire is met.

We want this or that. If we don't get what we want, we keep thinking about all that we don't have and we remain dissatisfied. If we do get what we want, we simply recreate the same thinking in our new circumstances. So, despite getting what we want, we still remain unhappy. Happiness can't be found when we are yearning for new desires.

Luckily, there is a way to be happy. It involves changing the emphasis of our thinking from what we want to what we have. Rather than wishing your spouse was different, try thinking about her wonderful qualities. Instead of complaining about your salary, be grateful that you have a job. Rather than wishing you were able to take a vacation to Hawaii, think of how much fun you have had close to home. The list of possibilities is endless! Each time you notice yourself falling into the "I wish life were different" trap, back off and start over. Take a breath and remember all that you have to be grateful. When you focus not on what you want, but on what you have, you end up getting more of what you want anyway. If you focus on the good qualities of your spouse, she'll be more loving. If you are grateful for your job rather than complaining about it, you'll do a better job, be more productive, and probably end up getting a raise anyway. If you focus on ways to enjoy yourself around home rather than waiting to enjoy yourself in Hawaii, you'll end up having more fun. If you ever do get to Hawaii, you'll be in the habit of enjoying yourself. And, if by some chance you don't, you'll have a great life anyway.

Make a note to yourself to start thinking more about what you have than what you want. If you do, your life will start appearing much better than before. For perhaps the first time in your life, you'll know what it means to feel satisfied.

自由飞翔

佚名

　　一个春风拂面的日子,一群年轻人正在放风筝。天空中满是各种颜色、形状和大小的风筝,犹如穿梭飞舞着的漂亮鸟儿。强劲有力的风吹着风筝,牵引线就控制着它们。

　　风筝并不是随风而去,而是迎风飘往高处。风的劲吹使它们摇晃着、扯拉着,但牵引线和笨重的尾翼让它们始终处于控制之中。它们挣扎着、抖动着,似乎在说:"放开我!放开我!我要自由!"就是在与风筝线抗争之时,它们也依然在优雅地飞翔着。终于,其中一只风筝成功地挣脱了线的束缚,它好像在说:"终于自由了,终于可以随风自由飞翔了。"

　　然而,没有束缚的自由让它完全处于风的无情摆布之下。它笨拙地坠落到地面,落在一堆乱草之中,线也缠在一丛枯死的灌木上了。"终于自由了"——自由到无力地躺在泥土中,自由到无助地任由风吹得满世界跑,自由到撞到第一个障碍物就搁浅,毫无生气可言。

　　有时候,我们与风筝是多么相似啊!上天让我们经历逆境,体验束缚,并定下规则约束我们,让我们从中成长起来,获得人生所需的力量。逆风而行时,束缚是不可或缺的。有些人强硬地抵制这些规则,那就永远也飞不到本可以达到的高度。只遵从部分规则,我们决不可能飞得很高。

　　每个人都飞到高处吧,同时也要认识到——某些令人恼怒的约束,实际上,是帮助我们攀升、飞跃和达成目标的强大力量。

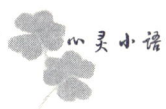
心灵小语

　　人们都渴望像断了线的风筝,挣脱束缚,在天际自由翱翔。可是一旦失去了约束,人们也会像风筝一样随风而逝,不知落到何处,最终弄得遍体鳞伤,失去了原来的模样。其实,那些束缚是帮助我们攀升的力量,让我们继续飞行、掌控未来的翅膀!

Free to Soar

Anonymous

One windy spring day, I observed young people having fun using the wind to fly their kites. Multicolored creations of varying shapes and sizes filled the skies like beautiful birds darting and dancing. As the strong winds gusted against the kites, a string kept them in check.

Instead of blowing away with the wind, they arose against it to achieve great heights. They shook and pulled, but the restraining string and the cumbersome tail kept them in tow, facing upward and against the wind. As the kites struggled and trembled against the string, they seemed to say, "Let me go! Let me go! I want to be free!" They soared beautifully even as they fought the restriction of the string. Finally, one of the kites succeeded in breaking loose. "Free at last," it seemed to say. "Free to fly with the wind."

Yet freedom from restraint simply put it at the mercy of an unsympathetic breeze. It fluttered ungracefully to the ground and landed in a tangled mass of weeds and string against a dead bush. "Free at last", free to lie powerless in the dirt, to be blown helplessly along the ground, and to lodge lifeless against the first obstruction.

How much like kites we sometimes are. Heaven gives us adversity and restrictions, rules to follow from which we can grow and gain strength. Restraint is a necessary counterpart to the winds of opposition. Some of us tug at the rules so hard that we never soar to reach the heights we might have obtained. We keep part of the commandment and never rise high enough to get our tails off the ground.

Let us each rise to the great heights, recognizing that some of the restraints that we may chafe under are actually the steadying force that helps us ascend and achieve.

彼岸无尽头，知足才常乐

佚名

很多人都认为，只有实现了自己既定的目标，我们才会幸福快乐。目标因人而异：有的人想拥有万贯家财；有的人想把令人厌烦的十几磅肉减掉；还有些人想觅到心仪的伴侣，获得一份较好的工作，开一部漂亮的车子，或拥有一份理想的职业，这些都可以是一个目标。不管你的目标何在，有一点是肯定的——只要达到了目标，你就可获得梦想中的安静与平和，你也一定会快乐、心满意足。

可事实往往并非如此。多数时候，当你达到彼岸时，仍不会满足，而且又会有新的憧憬。你总是劳心费神地去追求一个又一个目标，却对当前拥有的一切从不用心去欣赏和珍惜。每个人都有不满足现状的欲望，重要的是——头脑要时刻保持清醒。一方面，你的梦想和渴望使你的生活更丰富多彩。另一方面，这些欲望又驱使你越来越远离现有生活中的欢愉。

人们从远古时代开始便苦苦探究这一问题——我们如何能活在现实中。林林总总的幻想和憧憬始终在诱惑着我们——更多的荣耀、美貌和声誉。因而，这也是现代社会所面临的一个严峻挑战。若你知道感恩，就可真切地生活在现实中。

感恩是指对所拥有的一切和所处的人生境遇怀有感激之情，并懂得珍惜。你的心会因存有感恩而满溢愉悦，人生道路上的种种感受你都能亲身体验。如果你极力地将目光定格在现实当中，你就能体会到它的美妙之处。培养感恩之心的方法很多，建议你试试以下几种：

试想你丧失了目前正拥有的一切，你的生活将会如何？肯定会令你追悔不已——你是那么喜爱和珍惜这一切。

每天，将你感激的事物罗列出来，这样你就会意识到自己有多么幸运。天天都这么做，尤其在你觉得没什么可感激之时。或者，你也可以在睡前花几分钟对所拥有的一切表示感激。

花点时间向那些不如你幸运的人伸出援助之手,这样你可以对生活有更深刻的认识。

然而,你采取哪种方法学会感恩并不重要,努力去欣赏和珍惜正拥有的一切才是最为重要的,这样你就可以更幸福地享受当前的生活。

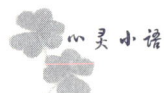 心灵小语

在这个国家或整个世界,并非人人都能做到,或不能对所有的事物心存一份满足。或许,如果我们对每天普通的事物都心存满足,必将有助于我们自己和其他人拥有更多丰富的收获,或者,至少会让我们多一份幸福感。

"There" Is No Better Than "Here"

Anonymous

Many people believe that they will be happy once they arrive at some specific goal they set for themselves. For some the goal may be **amassing**[1] a million dollars, for others losing those annoying ten-plus pounds, and for still others it is finding a **soulmate**[2]. It could be getting a better job, driving a nicer car, or pursuing a dream career. Whatever your "there" is, you may be convinced that once you arrive, you will finally find the peace you have always dreamed of; you will finally become fulfilled, happy, and content.

However, more often than not, once you arrive "there" you will still feel dissatisfied, and move your "there" vision to yet another point in the future. By always chasing after another "there", you are never really appreciating what you already have right "here". It is important for human beings to keep "sober-minded" about the age-old drive to look beyond the place where you now stand. On one hand, your life is enhanced by your dreams and **aspirations**[3]. On the other hand, these drives can pull you farther and farther from your enjoyment of your life right now.

People from the beginning of time have struggled with the question of how we can live in the present moment. And it is a challenge that has become particularly difficult in the modern world in which we are constantly lured by visions of greater **glory**[4], beauty, fame. If you learn to be grateful, you can fulfill the challenge of living in the present.

To be grateful means you are thankful for and appreciative of what you have and where you are on your path right now. Gratitude fills your heart with the joyful feeling and allows you to fully appreciate everything that arises on your path. As you strive to keep your focus on the present moment, you can experience the full wonder of "here". There are many ways to cultivate gratitude. Here are just a few suggestions you may wish to try:

Imagine what your life would be like if you lost all that you had. This will most surely remind you of how much you do appreciate it.

Make a list each day of all that you are grateful for, so that you can stay conscious daily of your blessings. Do this especially when you are feeling as though you have nothing to feel grateful for. Or spend a few minutes before you go to sleep giving thanks for all that you have.

Spend time offering **assistance**[5] to those who are less fortunate than you, so that you may gain perspective.

However you choose to learn gratitude is irrelevant. What really matters is that you create a space in your consciousness for appreciation for all that you have right now, so that you may live more joyously in your present moment.

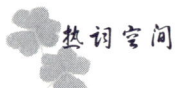热词空间

1. amass[əˈmæs] v. 收集;积聚(尤指财富)
2. soulmate n. [口]性情相投的人;心心相印的伙伴(尤指异性伙伴)
3. aspiration [ˌæspəˈreiʃən] n. 热情;渴望
4. glory [ˈglɔːri] n. 荣誉;光荣
5. assistance [əˈsistəns] n. 协助;援助;补助

第一卷

别让快乐远离我们

Don't Let Happiness Run Away From Us

快乐自有其道德基础。快乐的完整性让我们不得不考虑自己应该做什么样的人。当然，一些不怎么光彩的行为也会衍生快乐。但是，要想体验快乐，我们就得付出更多；正是快乐，让我们体会到了事物的可贵之处。真正的快乐需要做出选择，这些选择可以养成习惯从而形成性格。这是我们无法推脱的。

自由如歌的快乐

卡里·纪伯伦

快乐是一首自由的歌,但它不是自由。它是你们的欲望绽放的花朵,但不是它们的果实;它是深谷对高峰的呼唤,然而它既不深沉也不高耸;它是囚禁在笼中展翅的鸟儿,而不是环抱的空间。哦,的确,快乐是首自由的歌。我愿你们全心全意地歌唱它,不愿你们在歌唱时迷失自己的心。

你们年轻人中有一些追求快乐,好像它就是一切,他们已受到判决和谴责。我不会判决他们,也不会谴责他们,我会让他们去寻找。因为他们寻找的是快乐,然而也不单单是快乐;快乐有七个姐妹,她们中最小的也比她柔美。难道你们未曾听说有人在刨树根时发现了宝藏吗?

你们中有一些老年人遗憾地回忆快乐,好像在追悔酒醉后做的错事。但遗憾只会让心灵蒙上阴影,而不是一种惩罚。他们应以感恩之心回忆他们的快乐,好像回忆夏日的收获。但如果遗憾能给他们以慰藉,那就让他们得到安慰吧。

你们中一些人,既不是喜欢追寻的年轻人,又不是沉湎于回忆的老年人;他们在追寻和回忆的恐惧中逃避一切快乐,唯恐自己忽视或惹怒了心灵。

然而,在他们的前行中也有快乐。

因而,即使他们用颤抖的双手挖掘树根,他们也会找到宝藏。

请告诉我,谁敢惹怒灵魂呢?

夜莺会扰乱夜的寂静,萤火虫会惹恼繁星吗?你们的火焰和烟雾会拖累风吗?

你们以为灵魂是一汪止水,你们用一根木棍就可以搅乱吗?你们通常拒绝快乐,你们只是把快乐的欲望潜伏在内心中。

有谁知道,今天被忽略的事,明天会不会存在?甚至你们的身体也了解它的本性和合理需求,而不会被欺骗。

你们的身体是你们心灵的琴弦,它或奏出柔美的乐曲,或拨弄出混乱的噪音,全都在你。

现在你们扪心自问:"我们将怎样区别快乐中的善与恶呢?"去你们的田野和花园,你们就会明白蜜蜂的快乐在于采集花蜜,对于花朵而言,给蜜蜂提供花蜜就是快乐。因为蜜蜂视花朵为生命之泉,而花朵视蜜蜂为爱之使者,对于两者而言,蜜蜂与花朵,给予与接受的快乐是一种需要和狂喜的快乐。

奥菲里斯城的人们,尽情享受快乐吧,就像花朵和蜜蜂一样!

心灵小语

快乐是一首自由的歌,但它不是自由。它是你们的欲望绽放的花朵,但不是它们的果实;它是深谷对高峰的呼唤,然而它既不深沉也不高耸;它是囚禁在笼中展翅的鸟儿,而不是环抱的空间。

On Pleasure

Kahil Gibran

Pleasure is a freedom song, but it is not freedom. It is the blossoming of your desires; but it is not their fruit, it is a depth calling unto a height; but it is not the deep nor the high, it is the caged taking wing; but it is not space encompassed. Ay, in very truth, pleasure is a freedom song. And I fain would have you sing it with fullness of heart; yet I would not have you lose your hearts in the singing.

Some of your youth seek pleasure as if it was all, and they are judged and rebuked. I would not judge nor rebuke them. I would have them seek, for they shall find pleasure, but not her alone; seven are her sisters, and the least of them is more beautiful than pleasure. Have you not heard of the man who was digging in the earth for roots and found a treasure?

And some of your elders remember pleasures with regret like wrongs committed in drunkenness. But regret is the beclouding of the mind and not its chastisement. They should remember their pleasures with gratitude, as they would the harvest of a summer. Yet if it comforts them to regret, let them be comforted.

And there are among you those who are neither young to seek nor old to remember; and in their fear of seeking and remembering they **shun**[1] all pleasures, lest they neglect the spirit or offend against it.

But even in their **foregoing**[2] is their pleasure.

And thus they too find a treasure though they dig for roots with quivering hands.

But tell me, who is he that can offend the spirit?

Shall the nightingale offend the stillness of the night, or the **firefly**[3] the stars? And shall your flame or your smoke burden the wind?

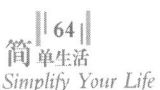

Thank you the spirit is a still pool which you can trouble with a staff? Oftentimes in denying yourself pleasure you do but store the desire in the recesses of your being.

Who knows but that which seem omitted today, waits for tomorrow? Even your body knows its heritage and its rightful need and will not be deceived.

And your body is the **harp**⁴ of your soul, and it is yours to bring forth sweet music from it or confused sounds.

And now you ask in your heart, "How shall we distinguish that which is good in pleasure from that which is not good?" Go to your fields and your gardens and you shall learn that it is the pleasure of the bee to gather honey of the flower, but it is also the pleasure of the flower to yield its honey to the bee, for to the bee a flower is a fountain of life, and to the flower a bee is a messenger of love, and to both, bee and flower, the giving and the receiving of pleasure is a need and an ecstasy.

People of Orphalese, be in your pleasures like the flowers and the bees.

1. shun [ʃʌn] *v.* 避开；避免
2. foregoing [fɔːˈgəuiŋ] *adj.* 在前的；前述的
3. firefly [ˈfaiflai] *n.* 萤火虫
4. harp [hɑːp] *n.* 竖琴

幸福之道

佚名

道德家们常说:幸福难求。唯有不明智地追寻,幸福才会遥不可及。蒙特卡洛城的赌徒们追求财富,而多数人却输掉钱财;但有人以另外的途径常获得财富。追求幸福亦如此。如果你想沉醉于酒精,以获得幸福感,只能暂时忘记烦扰。伊壁鸠鲁仅和同道者一起生活,且只吃干面包(奶酪,唯有节日才加点),也是他追求幸福的途径。在这方面,他是成功的,但这导致他体弱多病。而多数人需要旺盛的精力,这样追求快乐过于抽象,且操作性不强。但是,我想,除传奇之人和英雄人物外,无论你以何种准则来生活,都不应与幸福背道而驰。

很多人有着健康的身体和丰足的收入,这固然是幸福。然而,幸福却与他们无缘。就这一点来讲,似乎是生活原则出了问题。从某种意义上讲,任何有关生活的理论都不容佐证。动物和人类迥然相反。动物因本能而活,它们的快乐建立在客观条件是否得以满足的基础上。假如你养了只猫,它只要有东西吃,有温暖的地方睡,晚上可以时不时出去就很幸福了。人的需求也是以本能的满足为基础,但比起猫来,要复杂得多。处于文明社会,特别是讲英语的人们极其容易忘记这一点。人们定一个最高的目标,然后克制住所有与实现此目标相背驰的冲动。生意人过于急切赚大钱,可以牺牲健康和爱情。等到他腰缠万贯,除了奋斗历程可让他人效法,幸福并没有如期而至。很多贵妇人,尽管自身并不倾心于文学或艺术,却故作高雅,浪费时间去学习如何讲述流行的新书。而这些书的目的不是让人附庸风雅,而是带来读书的乐趣。

试着观察身边那些所谓的幸福男女,就会发现他们的相似之处。其中一点尤为重要:在多数情况下,生活本身是一种乐趣,借此可达成愿望。那些天生喜爱孩子的女人,能从相夫教子中得到快乐。艺术家、作家和科学家能够从工作的成就中获得快感。不过,还有很多低层次的幸福。诸如,在城里工作的许多人,到了周末,就在自家庭院里劳动,春天来临之时,就可全身心地享受劳动带来的如画风景。

在我看来，过去人们把幸福过于严肃化。以往，人们认为，要想拥有幸福，就必须拥有自己的生活原则或者宗教信仰。那些人认为自己的不快乐是源于低级理论，觉得唯有拥有一种较好的生活理论，他们的生活才会重焕生机，就像生病需要吃补药一样。但是，正常情况下，健康人不应以吃补药为生，不应把拥有理论作为生活幸福与否的标准。真正的幸福是微不足道的小事。假如一个事业有成的男人体贴妻子，爱护儿女，并时时刻刻满脸微笑，即使他们的生活原则糟糕透顶，他也是个快乐之人。相反，假如厌烦妻子，厌恶孩子的吵闹，怯于工作，整天巴望着日子快快溜走，那他就需要一种新的生活方式——改变饮食习惯，多运动等等，而不是新的生活理论。

人们坚信充满欢乐，远离痛苦的生活方式就等于幸福。实际上，这样反而减少了他们获得真正幸福的机会。如果懂得娱乐并不带来幸福，就会开始用不同的方式生活。其效果将是人生真正的转折点。

The Road to Happiness

Anonymous

It is a commonplace among moralists that you cannot get happiness by pursuing it. This is only true if you pursue it unwisely. Gamblers at Monte Carlo are pursuing money, and most of them lose it instead, but there are other ways of pursuing money, which often succeed. So it is with happiness. If you pursue it by means of drink, you are forgetting the hangover. Epicurus pursued it by living only in congenial society and eating only dry bread, supplemented by a little cheese on feast days. His method proved successful in his case, but he was a valetudinarian, and most people would need something more vigorous. For most people, the pursuit of happiness, unless supplemented in various ways, is too abstract and theoretical to be adequate as a personal rule of life. But I think that whatever personal rule of life you may choose it should not, except in rare and heroic cases, be incompatible with happiness.

There are a great many people who have all the material conditions of happiness, i.e. health and a sufficient income, and who, nevertheless, are profoundly unhappy. In such cases it would seem as if the fault must lie with a wrong theory as to how to live. In one sense, we may say that any theory as to how to live is wrong. We imagine ourselves more different from the animals than we are. Animals live on impulse, and are happy as long as external conditions are favorable. If you have a cat it will enjoy life if it has food and warmth and opportunities for an occasional night on the tiles. Your needs are more complex than those of your cat, but they still have their basis in instinct. In civilized societies, especially in English-speaking societies, this is too apt to be forgotten. People propose to themselves some one paramount objective, and restrain all impulses that do not minister to it. A businessman may be so anxious to grow rich that to this end he sacrifices health and private affections. When at last he has become rich, no pleasure remains to him except harrying other people by exhortations to imitate his noble example. Many rich ladies, although nature has not endowed them with any spontaneous pleasure in literature or art, decide to be thought cultured, and spend boring hours learning the right thing to say about fashionable new books that are written to give delight, not to afford opportunities for dusty snobbism.

If you look around at the men and women whom you can call happy, you will see that they all have certain things in common. The most important of these things is an activity which at most gradually builds up something that you are glad to see coming into existence. Women who take an instinctive pleasure in their children can get this kind of satisfaction out of bringing up a family. Artists and authors and men of science get happiness in this way if their own work seems good to them. But there are many humbler forms of the same kind of pleasure. Many men who spend their working life in the city devote their weekends to voluntary and unremunerated toil in their gardens, and when the spring comes, they experience all the joys of having created beauty.

The whole subject of happiness has, in my opinion, been treated too solemnly. It had been thought that man cannot be happy without a theory of life or a religion. Perhaps those who have been rendered unhappy by a bad theory may need a better theory to help them to recovery, just as you may need a tonic when you have been ill. But when things are normal a man should be healthy without a tonic and happy without a theory. It is the simple things that really matter. If a man delights in his wife and children, has success in work, and finds pleasure in the alternation of day and night, spring and autumn, he will be happy whatever his philosophy may be. If, on the other hand, he finds his wife fateful, his children's noise unendurable, and the office a nightmare; if in the daytime he longs for night, and at night sighs for the light of day, then what he needs is not a new philosophy but a new regimen—a different diet, or more exercise, or what not.

快乐之门

米尔德里德·克拉姆

快乐就像一枚鹅卵石突然掉入池塘中,激起一圈又一圈的涟漪,不断向外围扩散。正如史蒂文森说的,快乐是一种责任。

快乐没有确切的定义。快乐的理由成千上万,而关键并不在财富或健康。因为我们发现,乞丐、残疾人和所谓的失败者也能过得无比快乐。

快乐会有一种意想不到的收获。而保持快乐的心境是一种成就,是灵魂和性格的升华。事实上,追求快乐并非自私的表现,而是对自己和他人的一种责任。

郁闷就像一种传染病,人们往往对郁闷的人退避三舍。他们很快也会感到孤独、痛苦和难过。但是,有一种看似简单的治疗方法,虽然乍看似乎有些荒谬,如果你觉得不快乐,就假装快乐吧!

这个方法很管用,不久你就会发现,自己会吸引他人,而不是令人反感。你拥有一个以自己为中心的,日趋宽广的友好交际圈。这会是多么有益的事。

于是,假装的快乐就成了事实。你掌握了使心境平和的秘诀,并且,在愉悦他人的过程中,自己也变得忘乎所以了。

一旦意识到,保持快乐的心境是一种责任,并形成了习惯,它就能开启秘密花园的大门,那里云集着无数感激满怀的朋友。

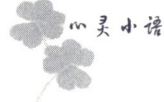

快乐带来的智慧存在于清晰的心灵感觉中,不因忧虑担心而困惑,不因绝望厌烦而迟钝,不因惶恐而出现盲点。请把快乐之门打开,把心放飞,让它在蔚蓝的天际中翱翔,享受这份来自广阔的快乐!

The Happy Door

Mildred Cram

Happiness is like a pebble dropped into a pool to set in motion an ever-widening circle of **ripples**[1]. As Stevenson has said, being happy is a duty.

There is no exact definition of the word—happiness. Happy people are happy for all sorts of reasons. The key is not wealth or physical well-being, since we find beggars, invalids and so-called failures that are **extremely**[2] happy.

Being happy is a sort of unexpected dividend. But staying happy is an accomplishment, a triumph of soul and character. It is not selfish to strive for it. It is, indeed, a duty to us and others.

Being unhappy is like an infectious disease; it causes people to shrink away from the sufferer. He soon finds himself alone, miserable and embittered. There is, however, a cure so simple as to seem, at first glance, ridiculous: If you don't feel happy, pretend to be!

It works. Before long you will find that instead of repelling people, you attract them. You discover how deeply rewarding it is to be the center of wider and wider circles of good will.

Then the make-believe becomes a reality. You possess the secret of peace of mind, and can forget yourself in being of service to others.

Being happy, once it is realized as a duty and established as a habit, opens doors into unimaginable gardens thronged with grateful friends.

1. ripple ['ripl] *n.* 波纹
2. extrmely [iks'tri:mli] *adv.* 极端地；非常地

做一个乐观者

佚名

如果你转变思想——从悲观主义者变为乐观主义者——你就能改变你的人生。

——克雷普·萨弗兰

你所看到的是半杯水,还是杯中空的一半呢?你看见的是炸面包圈,还是其间的空洞呢?当研究人员仔细研究积极思维的效应时,这些陈词滥调陡然间就都成了科学性的问题。研究表明,乐观能使人更快乐、健康和成功。悲观则相反,它使人绝望、病态和失败,并与消沉、孤寂和痛苦的胆怯紧密相连。如果我们能教导人们更加积极地思考,就如同给那些心理疾病患者注射了预防疫苗。

习惯固然重要,但真正影响你成功的,却是你是否有成功的信念。从某种程度上说,这是因为乐观者和悲观者在面对同样的挑战和失望时,会用截然不同的态度来处理。当事情进展不顺时,悲观者会责备自己,他可能会说:"我并不擅长这个,我永远都是失败的。"而乐观者则会去找寻疏漏之处。不论是消极心态,还是积极心态,都是一种能够自我实现的预料。如果人们觉得希望渺茫,就不会努力获得成功所必须的技能。

自我控制能力是成功的试金石。乐观者觉得能掌控自己的命运。如果事情变得糟糕,他会迅速做出反应,寻找解决方案,制定新的行动计划,还会四处请教。悲观者则听任命运的摆布,行动迟缓。他认为事已至此,无能为力,固而不会寻求赐教。许多研究表明,悲观者的无助感会破坏其身体的自然防御体系,即免疫体系;他们无法照顾好自己;消极被动,禁不住生活的风雨;不论做什么,他都会担心身体不好或者会有其他不幸;他还会吞吃垃圾食品,拒绝锻炼,不听信于医生,一再放纵酗酒。

　　人们大多都集悲观和乐观于一身,但会偏向于其中一方。这是从小受母亲的影响而形成的一种思维模式。父母无数次地警告或鼓励,消极或积极的话语是这种思维模式形成的根源。太多的"不能"和危险的警告让孩子感到无所适从,备感恐惧——这样就形成了悲观主义。虽然悲观主义很难克服,但也不是全然不能克服。

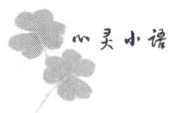

　　乐观者往往能看到事情积极的一面,懂得"塞翁失马,焉知非福"的道理,而悲观者却总是在阴暗面徘徊,"杞人忧天",终日郁郁寡欢,忧愁至极,最终了无生趣地度过一生。读完这篇文章后,你是否明白了其中的道理,那你知道该怎样做了吗?

Be an Optimist

Anonymous

If you change your mind— from pessimism to optimism— you can change your life.

— Claipe Safran

Do you see the glass as half–full rather than half empty? Do you keep your eye upon the doughnut, not upon the hole? Suddenly these clichs are scientific questions, as **researchers**[1] scrutinize the power of positive thinking. Research is proving that optimism can help you to be happier, healthier and more successful. Pessimism leads, by contrast, to hopelessness, sickness and failure, and is linked to depression, loneliness and painful shyness. If we could teach people to think more positively, it would be like **inoculating**[2] them against these mental ills.

Your habits count but the belief that you can succeed affects whether or not you will. In part, that's because optimists and pessimists deal with the same challenges and disappointments in very different ways. When things go wrong the pessimist tends to blame himself. "I'm not good at this." "I always fail." He would say. But the optimist looks for loopholes. Negative or positive, it was a self–fulfilling prophecy. If people feel hopeless they don't bother to acquire the skills they need to succeed.

A sense of control is the litmus test for success. The optimist feels in control of his own life. If things are going badly, he acts quickly, looking for solutions, forming a new plan of action, and reaching out for advice. The pessimist feels like fate's plaything and moves slowly. He doesn't seek advice, since he assumes nothing can be done. Many studies suggest that the pessimist's feeling of helplessness **undermines**[3] the body's natural defenses, the **immune**[4] system. Research has found that the pessimist doesn't take good care of himself. Feeling passive and unable to dodge life's blows, he expects ill health and other misfortunes, no matter what he does. He munches on junk food, avoids exercise, ignores the doctor, has another drink.

Most people are a mix of optimism and pessimism, but are inclined in one direction or the other. It is a pattern of thinking learned at our mothers' knees. It grows out of thousands of cautions or encouragements, negative statements or positive ones. Too many "don't" and warnings of danger can make a child feel incompetent, fearful—and pessimistic. Pessimism is a hard habit to break—but it can be done.

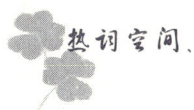

1. scrutiniae ['skrutinaiz] *v.* 细察
2. inoculate [i'nɔkjuleit] *v.* 接种；嫁接
3. undermine [ˌʌndə'main] *v.* 破坏
4. immune [i'mju:n] *adj.* 免疫的

我们对幸福的追求

佚名

我们四处追逐幸福,而幸福其实就在我们身边。

一天,我问哥哥伊恩:"你感到幸福吗?"他回答说:"可以说幸福,也可以说不幸福,这要看你指什么了。"

"那你告诉我,"我说,"最近一次你感到幸福是什么时候?"

"1967年4月,"他答道。

我真不该对一个游戏生活的人提出这么严肃的问题。但伊恩的回答却给了我一个启示:我们想到的幸福时刻通常是一些非同寻常的事,一种纯粹的快乐——但是随着年龄的增长,这种快乐好像越来越少了。

对一个孩子来说,幸福有着梦幻般的色彩。记得我曾在新鲜的干草丛中捉迷藏;在树林里玩"警察与小偷";在学校的戏剧里扮演有台词的角色。当然,孩子也有情绪低落的时候。但是,因为赢得一场比赛,或得了一辆新车,他们会毫不掩饰地快乐到极点。

到了青少年时期,幸福观逐渐转变。突然间,幸福就建立在激动、爱情、名气甚至是脸上的青春痘能否在晚会前消失这样的事上。我清楚地记得,大家都去参加一个舞会,而我未被邀请时的痛苦。但也记得,在另一次活动中,我意外地与一个貌似约翰·特拉沃尔塔的人共舞时的兴奋。

成年后,心灵深处最令人喜悦的是生育和爱情,婚姻同时也带来了责任和安逸。爱情可能会消逝,性爱也不总是如意,心爱的人可能会死去。对于成人来说,幸福很复杂。

字典里幸福的定义是"幸运"或"好运",但我认为幸福更好的定义是"感受快乐的能力"。更多地享受我们拥有的一切,我们就能更多地享受幸福。但是,爱与被爱,友人相伴,简单的生活,甚至健康的体魄,这些细碎的快乐却很容易被我们忽视。

我合计了一下昨日的幸福时光,首先我盖上最后一个饭盒,独享整个房间,感受无比的幸福。然后,整个早上,我都在写字而无人打扰,这是我乐于做的。孩子们回到家,我又享受着寂静一天后的热闹。

不久,再次恢复宁静,我和丈夫享受另一种快乐——亲热。有时候只要想到他需要我,就能给我带来快乐。

你永远不会知道幸福下一次会在什么时候出现。当我问起朋友,什么能给他们带来幸福时,有些人会提到一些看似微不足道的小事。"我讨厌购物,"一个朋友说,"但有些健谈的售货员的确令我很开心。"另一个朋友喜欢接电话,"每次电话一响,我就知道有人想我了。"

我喜欢开车的刺激。一天,我停下来,让一辆学校班车拐到路边。那个司机咧嘴一笑,会意地竖起大拇指。我们都是这个世界上的飚车一族,这让我很高兴。

我们都有过类似的经历,但很少有人能意识到这就是幸福。

心理学家告诉我们,幸福既需要愉快的休闲时间,也需要满意的工作。我的曾祖母让我很疑惑,她养育了14个孩子,还要给别人洗衣服,做其他一些家务杂活。但她有一个亲密的朋友和和睦的家。或许,这已使她很满足了。如果说她因自己拥有的一切感到幸福,或许是因为她并不希望生活是另一番样子。

另一方面,我们因为有太多的选择及想在各个领域成功的压力,让我们把幸福变成"必须得到"的一种东西。我们自私地以为我们有"权"得到它,这也是我们痛苦的根源。所以我们去追求幸福,并将它同财富和成功联系起来,而没有意识到拥有它的人并不一定更幸福。

对我们来说,幸福是复杂多样的,但获得幸福的方式却相同。幸福不是发生在我们周围的事——而是我们如何去看待周围发生的事。这是变不利为有利,化挫折为激励的秘诀。幸福并非是乞求我们未得到的,而是享受我们此刻所拥有的一切。

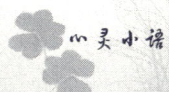

幸福其实很简单,是一种简单的生活,又不缺乏味道;是一种乏味的生活,又不缺烦琐;是一种烦琐的生活,又不缺宜便;是一种宜便的生活,又不缺快乐;是一种快乐的生活,但也会有烦恼……但是总而言之,幸福的生活,人人都有资格追求,它属于每一个人!

Our Pursuit of Happiness

Anonymous

We chase after it, when it is waiting all about us.

"Are you happy?" I asked my brother, Ian, one day. "Yes. No. It depends on what you mean," he said.

"Then tell me," I asked, "when was the last time you think you were happy?"

"April 1967," he said.

It served me right for putting a serious question to someone who has joked his way through life. But Ian's answer reminded me that when we think about happiness, we usually think of something extraordinary, a pinnacle of sheer delight—and those pinnacles seem to get rarer the older we get.

For a child, happiness has a magical quality. I remember making hide-outs in newly cut hay, playing cops and robbers in the woods, getting a speaking part in the school play. Of course, kids also experience lows, but their delight at such peaks of pleasure as winning a race or getting a new bike is unreserved.

In the teenage years the concept of happiness changes. Suddenly it's conditional on such things as excitement, love, popularity and whether that zit will clear up before prom night. I can still feel the agony of not being invited to a party that almost everyone else was going to. But I also recall the ecstasy of being plucked from obscurity at another event to dance with a John Travolta look-alike.

In adulthood the things that bring profound joy—birth, love, marriage also—bring responsibility and the risk of loss. Love may not last, sex isn't always good, loved ones die. For adults, happiness is complicated.

My dictionary defines happy as "lucky" or "fortunate," but I think a better definition of happiness is "the capacity for enjoyment." The more we can enjoy what we have, the happier we are. It's easy to overlook the pleasure we get from loving and being loved, the

company of friends, the freedom to live where we please, and even good health.

I added up my little moments of pleasure yesterday. First there was sheer bliss when I shut the last lunch-box and had the house to myself. Then I spent an uninterrupted morning writing, which I love. When the kids came home, I enjoyed their noise after the quiet of the day.

Later, peace descended again, and my husband and I enjoyed another pleasure—intimacy. Sometimes just the knowledge that he wants me can bring me joy.

You never know where happiness will turn up next. When I asked friends what made them happy, some mentioned seemingly insignificant moments. "I hate shopping," one friend said. "but there's a clerk who always chats and really cheers me up." Another friend loves the telephone "Every time it rings, I know someone is thinking about me."

I get a thrill from driving. One day I stopped to let a school bus turn onto a side road. The driver grinned and gave me thumbs up sign. We were two allies in a world of mad motorists. It made me smile.

We all experience moments like these. Too few of us register them as happiness.

Psychologists tell us that to be happy we need a blend of enjoyable leisure time and satisfying work. I doubt that my great-grandmother, who raised 14 children and took in washing, had much of either. She did have a network of close friends and family, and maybe this was what fulfilled her. If she was happy with what she had, perhaps it was because she didn't expect life to be very different.

We, on the other hand, with so many choices and such pressure to succeed in every area, have turned happiness into one more thing we "gotta have." We're so self-conscious about our "right" to it that it's making us miserable. So we chase it and equate it with wealth and success, without noticing that the people who have those things aren't necessarily happier.

While happiness may be more complex for us, the solution is the same as ever. Happiness isn't about what happens to us—it's about how we perceive what happens to us. It's the knack of finding a positive for every negative, and viewing a setback as a challenge. It's not wishing for what we don't have, but enjoying what we do possess.

别让快乐远离我们

佚名

一个大学生曾告诉我:"我不需要快乐——我只要成功。"

这是一个奇怪的思想对比。她不需要快乐——"只要成功"。她将这两者对立起来。

对学生而言,今天的言就是明天的行。他们所说的话很具有代表性,每个人都会努力奋斗,只是这种努力往往不易觉察。

记得上大学时,校报上有一篇文章的标题是这样的:"为什么我们不快乐?"这个标题的意思是:我们的生活缺少快乐。然而,我们的生活中有快乐,至少,我们仍在寻找快乐。像那个追求成功的学生一样,许多人宁愿放弃快乐,这是为什么呢?

为了确保周一的工作进度,我在周日也常常加班。这实际上是提前对未来一周的工作感到焦虑——担心会发生意想不到的麻烦或觉得自己在某些方面做不好。但我通常在正常上班的日子做得很不错。我担心的很多事从未发生过。

快乐自有其道德基础。快乐的完整性让我们不得不考虑自己应该做什么样的人。当然,一些不怎么光彩的行为也会衍生快乐。但是,要想体验快乐,我们就得付出更多;正是快乐,让我们体会到了事物的可贵之处。

真正的快乐需要做出选择,这些选择可以养成习惯从而形成性格。这是我们无法推脱的。

因此,获取真正快乐的首要一步就是减少忧虑——这个关键的第一步能让我们远离忧虑。它要求我们勇于接受毫无预想的一切,坦然面对生活中的所有烦恼。

心灵小语

快乐是一种心境,跟财富、环境、年龄无关,功名利禄只能给我们短暂的快乐。唯有纯净的心灵,对生活的博爱,才能给我们永恒的喜悦。一个人要想获得真正的快乐不是获得成功,增加财富,而是降低欲望,品味现在……

Don't Let Happiness Run Away From Us

Anonymous

A college student once told me: "I don't need to be happy—just successful." It's an odd juxtaposition. She needn't be happy—"just successful". She places one in opposition to the other.

Students are today's expressions of tomorrow's practices. Their words can be the visible signs of the less visible struggles encountered by us all.

I have a memory from my own undergraduate years of a headline in my campus newspaper: "Why Aren't We Happy?" As the headline suggests, we fell short of leading joyful lives. Yet at least happiness was still on the agenda. What underlies the tendency of many of us, like my success-seeking student, to give up genuinely trying?

I've often failed to enjoy Sunday because of my schedule on Monday. At bottom, it was simply anticipatory anxiety over the work of the week ahead—fear that there would be unexpected complications or that I would fail to measure up in some way. Usually, when Monday came, I did quite well. Much of what I worried about never happened.

Joy has its own moral underpinning. There's a completeness to joy that does not allow us to exclude our sense of the person we should be. Pleasure is certainly possible in less-than-honorable actions. But the experience of joy requires more; it is pleasure taken in worthy things.

True joy requires choices that develop into habits that evolve into character. And that's work we can't delegate.

The essential first step is trying to live a less fearful life—one that avoids collapsing life's possibilities before exploring them. It entails welcoming uncertainty and comfortable incompleteness.

感受快乐

佚名

有几种方法可以达到快乐的境界呢?

1. 快乐不是目标,而是一次旅程。如果你在旅程中寻找快乐,那过程就变成终点,而且是你生命中受益匪浅、意义深远的终点。

2. 快乐的地方就在此处,快乐的时刻就在此时。停留在此处,并抓住此刻,你就是快乐的。

3. 快乐首先体现在精神上,而后是身体上。为了使身体上的快乐更加丰盈,你必须要做到气定神闲,毫无烦忧。宁可吃饭的时候无肉,也不要让心中满是负担。

4. 快乐与忧愁是相互对立的,此消彼长。从忧愁中解脱出来,才能享受到快乐。

5. 快乐是五块饼和两条鱼;放出的越多,得到的越多。与他人分享你的快乐,你会更快乐。

6. 如果你心里的愿望很容易就得到满足,那你的快乐也会很快结束。为了能延长你的快乐,就必须要有未完成的愿望。

7. 当你快乐时,你会感到满足;不开心时,也要保持心情舒畅。经常富于激情,快乐就会成为根深蒂固的习惯。

8. 快乐是一件非常奇怪的事。当你召唤它、命令它、恳求它时,它却不出来。但当你假装不关心它时,它却又来讨好你、依偎着你、与你共处。与快乐打交道,你需要"欲擒故纵"。

9. 快乐四处飘荡。试图抓住它,是愚昧又无用的。你需要制造新的快乐,以使快乐接连不断。

10. 你能获得的最大快乐,就是意识到快乐并不是你的必需。

心灵小语

快乐有时就像在天上飞的风筝一样,虽然有时你看不见,线却在你手中,它就不会飞远。只要你愿意,快乐就会随时围绕着你,直到永远。

Ten Ways to Happiness

Anonymous

How many ways are there to reach the state of being happy?

1. Happiness is not an aim, but a journey. If you seek for pleasure in the course of the journey, the course will become a destination, and what's more, it will be a prolonged, boundlessly beneficial destination for all your life.

2. The happy place is this place, and the happy moment is this moment. Remain standing here, seize the present moment, and you will be happy.

3. Happiness is mental before it is physical. In order to be physically happy to the full, you must first feel at ease and be free of worry. It is better to eat without meat than to have a load on your mind.

4. Happiness is the opposite of unhappiness; the decline of the one means the growth of the other. Release yourself from the unhappy mood and you will be happy.

5. Happiness is a matter of five cakes of bread and two fishes; the more you give out the more you will get back. Share your happiness with others and you will enjoy it most.

6. If your heart's desire is easily satisfied, your happiness will soon come to an end. In order that your happiness may last, you have to leave some of your desires unfulfilled.

7. When you are happy, you feel contented. You should also feel contented, when you are unhappy. Be always full of zest and happiness will become an inveterate habit.

8. Happiness is a very strange thing. It will not turn up when you beckon it, call it, and solicit it. But when you feign complete indifference, it will fawn upon you, lean close to you and live with you. In dealing with happiness, you should adopt the strategy of leaving it at large the better to apprehend it.

9. Happiness is drifting from place to place. It is unwise as well as futile to try to retain it. You have got to keep on making new happiness, so that one happiness follows in the wake of another.

10. The greatest happiness you can gain is realizing that you are not necessarily in need of it.

幸福的真谛

佚名

我住在好莱坞迪斯尼乐园,那里全年阳光普照。你可能认为生活在那么富于魅力,充满乐趣的地方,一定比其他地方的人更幸福。如果这么想,你可能对幸福的真谛有些误解。

很多聪明的人仍将幸福等同于乐趣。其实,乐趣和幸福的共同之处极少,或者说根本就没有。乐趣是行为过程中的感受,而幸福是我们行为过后的感受,它是一种更为深刻、持久的感情。

人们坚信充满欢乐,远离痛苦的生活方式就等于幸福。实际上,这样反而减少了他们获得真正幸福的机会。如果欢乐和愉快等同幸福,那痛苦就等同不幸。其实恰恰相反,多数情况下,能带来幸福的事物往往包含诸多痛苦。

所以说,许多人所逃避的艰难困苦恰恰是真正幸福的源泉。这些人害怕那些必定会带来痛苦的事情,如结婚、抚养子女、提高专业技能、承担宗教义务、社会服务或慈善事业,提升自我等。

尽管一个单身者对约会越来越不感兴趣,但当你问他为什么还不想结婚时,如果他很诚实,就会告诉你,他怕承担责任。因为承担责任确实是一件痛苦的事情。独身生活充满着乐趣、冒险和激情。婚姻虽也有如此体验,却大为逊色。

同样,选择不要孩子的夫妻都有一种观点,即宁可要不痛苦的欢乐,也不要痛苦的幸福。他们可以随时出去吃饭、旅游,想睡到多晚就睡多晚。而有孩子的夫妻,睡上一整晚,或有三天假期,算是幸运的了。我想,任何夫妇都不会用"乐趣"这个词来形容抚养孩子。

美丽英文
Beautiful English

但是,不要孩子的夫妇永远也体会不到,拥抱孩子或晚上给孩子掖好被子时的愉悦。他们永远不知道,看着孩子长大或者逗弄儿孙的乐趣。

然而,这些形式的乐趣在任何意义上都称不上是我所谓的幸福。写作、抚养孩子、增进与妻子的感情、为社会做些善事——这些给我带来的幸福远比娱乐带来的乐趣要多。要知道,娱乐是转瞬即逝的。

了解并接受真正的幸福与娱乐毫不相干,我们就能获得最大限度的解放。它解放了时间:现在我们能集中更多的时间去从事那些能带给我们真正幸福的活动;它解放了金钱:买一辆新车或一些时尚的衣物并不能增加我们的幸福;它把我们从嫉妒中解放出来:我们懂得,那些曾被我们确信幸福的富豪权贵们,只不过是享受了太多的娱乐,事实上或许毫无幸福可言。

我们如果懂得娱乐并不带来幸福,就会开始用不同的方式生活。其效果将是人生真正的转折点。

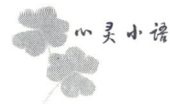
心灵小语

乐趣是行为过程中的感受,而幸福是我们行为过后的感觉,它是一种更为深刻、持久的感情。我们要懂得把握幸福,若是等到某些东西的出现,才会感到幸福,那你永远若有所失,永远也体会不到真正的幸福。

The Essence of Happiness

Anonymous

I live in the land of Disney, Hollywood and year round sun. You may think people in such a glamorous, fun filled place are happier than others. If so, you have some mistakes about the nature of happiness.

Many intelligent people still equate happiness with fun. The truth is that fun and happiness have little or nothing in common. Fun is what we experience during an act. Happiness is what we experience after an act. It is deeper, more abiding emotion.

The way people cling to the belief that a fun filled, pain free life equals happiness actually **diminishes**[1] their chances of ever attaining real happiness. If fun and pleasure are equated with happiness, then pain must be equated with unhappiness. But in fact, the opposite is true: More times than not, things that lead to happiness involve some pain.

As a result, many people avoid the very **endeavors**[2] that are the source of tree happiness. They fear the pain inevitably brought by such things as marriage, raising children, professional achievement, religious commitment, civic or **charitable**[3] work, and self-improvement.

Ask a bachelor why he resists marriage even though he finds dating to be less and less satisfying. If he's honest, he will tell you that he is afraid of making a commitment. For commitment is in fact quite painful. The single life is filled with fun, adventure, excitement. Marriage has such movement, but they are not its most distinguishing features.

Similarly, couples who choose not to have children are deciding in favor of painless fun over painful happiness. They can dine out whenever they want, travel wherever they want and sleep as late as they want. Couples with infant children are lucky to get a whole night's sleep or a three-day vacation. I don't know any parents would choose the word fun to describe raising children.

But couples who decide not to have children never experience the pleasure of hugging them or tucking them into bed at night. They never know the joy of watching a child grow up or of playing with a grandchild.

But these forms of fun do not contribute in any way to my happiness. More difficult endeavors—writing, raising children, creating deep relationship with my wife, trying to do good in the world—will bring me more happiness than can ever be found in fun, that least permanent things.

Understanding and accepting that true happiness has nothing to do with fun is one of the most liberating realizations we can ever come to. It liberates time: now we can devote more hours to activities that can genuinely increase our happiness. It liberates money: buying that new car or those fancy clothes that will do nothing to increase our happiness now seems pointless. And it liberates us from envy: we now understand that all those rich and glamorous people we were so sure are happy because they are always having so much fun actually may not be happy at all.

The moment we understand that fun does not bring happiness, we began to lead our lives differently. The effect can be, quite **literally**[4], life transforming.

1. diminish [di'miniʃ] v. 使(减少);使(变小)
2. endeavor [in'devə] n. 努力;尽力
3. charitable ['tʃæritəbl] adj. 仁慈的
4. literally ['litərəli] adv. 照字面意义;逐字地

生活的乐趣

佚名

生活的乐趣源自美好的情感,相信这些情感,让它们如鸟儿般自由地在天空翱翔。生活中的快乐永远不能伪装得来。拥有快乐生活的人无须言语,就会用快乐感染他人。他们将快乐释放,让快乐发光,用快乐的光芒照耀他人的生活,就像鸟儿奉献自己的歌声一样。

仅仅为追求生活的乐趣而努力,永远不会成功。它如同幸福一样,只会跟随有更高追求的人。它是伟大而简单的生活的附属品,生活的乐趣源自我们对其的投入,而非索取。

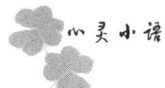
心灵小语

快乐是你对生活的态度,快乐是你对生活的理解。"知足者常乐"还是"不知足者常乐"?每个人都有不同的理解。只要有一颗平常的心,看世事无常,看沧桑变化,任你狂风又冷雨,我自逍遥。从生活的每个细节,从万世万物的每一点变化,感受生命的意义。存在,就是快乐的。生活,也就是快乐的。

The Joy of Living

Anonymous

The joy in living comes from having fine emotions, trusting them, giving them the freedom of a bird in the open. Joy in living can never be assumed as a pose, or put on from the outside as a **mask**[1]. People who have this joy don't need to talk about it; they radiate it. They just live out their joy and let it **splash**[2] its sunlight and glow into other lives as naturally as bird sings.

We can never get it by working for it directly. It comes, like happiness, to those who are aiming at something higher. It is a **byproduct**[3] of great, simple living. The joy of living comes from what we put into living, not from what we seek to get from it.

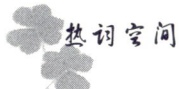

1. mask [mɑːsk] *n.* 面具；掩饰
2. splash [splæʃ] *v.* 溅；泼；溅湿
3. byproduct *n.* 副产品

排遣压力，享受生活

佚名

  假期又来临了。大部分人都很期待它的到来。但是由于我们将自己沉浸在整个假期中——聚会、购物、烹饪、串亲戚，清帐——一切我们所盼的，聚在一起的快乐和温暖的感觉，常常会带来少许的压力和疲倦。

  在激情时刻做到没有压迫感几乎是不可能的，这里有一些方法可以使这些压迫感保持平衡。考虑以下几个小点，会给你的假期增添些许快乐。

  ——在假期时还要坚持锻炼，即使强度比平常稍稍减轻一点。

  ——努力多吃健康食品。

  在聚会和其他假期活动的间隙要多休息。

  ——留心来自心底的声音。

  你是否错过了一个儿时的特别假期仪式？你能否把它安排在你现在的假期日程中？

  ——学会宽容。

  记住每一个排着长队购物的人都会像你一样担心时间。（不过最好可以选择网上购物！）

  ——懂得取舍。

  你不能做所有想做的事，如果你尝试一下，其实并不开心。

  ——提前预算假期的开支。

  列一个花销清单，并遵循它。

  ——记住饮酒只会使你有感觉舒服和压力减轻的幻觉。

  饮酒时需要注意的就是适度——特别是当许多压力同时出现时的假期。

  ——在家庭聚会中避开艰难或敏感的话题。

——施与他人少许救济。

救济一个贫穷家庭。给穷困的孩子一些玩具。记住施与是假期的真正快乐。

如果你的家庭有些变化,或是因为一些原因你不能与你爱的人共度假期,去寻找与你处于同样境地的人们共度一个特别的假期。

——向朋友倾诉,或者,如果需要的话,找一位临床医学家,把你假期里的郁闷与压力告诉他。

通常,将自己的心事吐露出来,有助于缓解消极的情绪,而且交流可以给你提供一个缓解压力的环境。

——感激你所拥有的一切。

心灵小语

压力,人人都会遇到,可是要怎么解决呢?可以给自己一个空间,付出一些时间,用一些其他的活动或爱好来调动内心的轻松、快乐的情绪,如读一本令人捧腹的小说,看一场激动人心的电影,听一场气势磅礴的交响音乐会,或者干脆在家里亲自调理出一顿美味佳肴。排遣生活的压力,让我们轻装上阵!

12 Ways to Minimize Stress

Anonymous

It's holiday again. Most of us look forward to it. But as we **immerse**[1] ourselves in the holiday season—the parties, the shopping, the cooking, the relatives, the bills—what we were hoping for, fun and warm feelings of togetherness, often turns out to be little more than stress and **fatigue**[2].

Although it is nearly impossible not to experience some increase in stress during this hectic time, there are ways to help keep stress levels manageable. Consider the following tips to help make your holidays a little brighter.

—Continue to exercise during the holidays, even if it's less than your usual **regimen**[3].

—Try to eat healthy foods.

Relax between parties and other holiday obligations.

—Be aware of what's going on inside of you.

Are you missing a special holiday ritual from your childhood? Can you incorporate it in to your current holiday plans?

—Practise tolerance.

Remember that everyone in those long shopping lines is just as pressed for time as you are. (Better yet shop online!)

—Prioritize, prioritize, prioritize.

You cannot do it all, and if you try, you surely will not enjoy yourself.

—Budget your holiday spending money ahead of time.

Write down your spending list and stick to it.

—Remember that drinking alcohol only gives the illusion of feeling better and less stressed.

It is important to drink only in **moderation**⁴—particularly during the holidays when many other stresses are present.

—Avoid bringing up difficult or sensitive subject matter at family gatherings.

—Give to someone less fortunate.

Adopt a needy family. Donate toys for underprivileged children. Remember that giving is the true spirit of the holidays.

—If you are from a displaced family, or for some reason cannot be with your loved ones during the holidays, seek out others in the same situation and plan a special gathering.

—Talk to a friend, or, if needed, a **therapist**⁵, about your holiday blues and stress.

Often, just verbalizing your thoughts will help alleviate the negative feelings, and the interchange can provide you with some stress-relief solutions.

—Be thankful for all you have.

1. immerse [i'mə:s] v. 沉浸；使陷入
2. fatigue [fə'ti:g] n. 疲劳；疲乏
3. regimen ['redʒimen] n. 摄生法；政体；政权
4. moderation [ˌmɔdə'reiʃən] n. 适度
5. therapist ['θerəpist] n. 临床医学家

幸福生活的建议

佚名

1. 犯错没关系

每个人都会犯错。即使犯了错,我仍然是一个优秀的、有价值的人。犯错后,没必要惴惴不安。我一直都在努力,即使犯了错,我还是会继续努力。我能正确对待犯错,别人犯错也没什么大不了的。既然我会接受自己犯错,也就会接受别人犯错。

2. 并非人人都得爱我

不是每个人都得爱我,或者喜欢我。我不必喜欢我认识的每一个人,那么为什么其他人都应该喜欢我呢?我很乐意被人喜欢或被人爱,但如果有人不喜欢我,我仍然会活得很好,也觉得自己很好。我不能强求别人喜欢我,正如别人也不能强求我喜欢他。我不需要总是被认可。如果别人不认同我,我仍然会活得很好。

3. 不必事必躬亲

如果事情与我所想象的不同,我也照样生活。我会接受事情本来的样子,接受人们本来的面貌,也接受真实的自我。如果我不能让事情成为我想要的样子,也没必要不安。我没有理由要喜欢一切事物。即使我不喜欢它,仍能与之共存。

4. 对自己的每一天负责

我对自己的感觉和自己所做的事负责。没有人能影响我的感觉。如果我浑浑噩噩地过了一天,是我对自己的放任;如果我某天过得很充实,是自己态度积极,应受嘉奖。其他人没有义务做出改变来让我感觉更好。我才是掌握自己命运的人。

5. 出了问题我能处理

我不需要时刻担心事情会出错。事情一般都会顺利进行，就是不能顺利进行时，我也能处理好。我不需要把时间浪费在不必要的焦虑上。天不会塌下来，一切都会好的。

6. 我能行

我不需要别人来帮忙处理问题，我能行。我能照顾好自己，能自己做出决定，能独立思考。我不需要别人来照顾我。

7. 我能随机应变

一件事的做法不止一种，不止一个人有行得通的好办法，也没有哪一种方法是万全之策。每个人都有好主意。有些可能对我更有帮助，但是每个人的观点都有可取之处，每个人都可以想出一些好办法。

要想获得幸福，就要有一个好的心态和一种健康的人生观！人生苦短，不必计较太多。能够放下一切，你就会获得真正的幸福！不要怨天尤人，只要尽力就可以了！我们在时空之中是非常渺小的，在人类历史上只是一个匆匆过客而已，只要珍惜生命，做到无怨无悔就很好！

Good Advice to Help You Live Happily

Anonymous

1. It is Okay to Make Mistakes

Making mistakes is something we all do, and I am still a fine and worthwhile person when I make them. There is no reason for me to get upset when I make a mistake. I am trying, and if I make a mistake, I am going to continue trying. I can handle making a mistake. It is okay for others to make mistakes, too. I will accept mistakes in myself and also mistakes that others make.

2. Everybody Doesn't Have to Love Me

Not everybody has to love me or even like me. I don't necessarily like everybody, I know, so why should everybody else like me? I enjoy being liked and being loved, but if somebody doesn't like me, I will still be okay and still feel like I am an okay person. I cannot make somebody like me, anymore than somebody can get me to like them. I don't need approval all the time. If someone does not approve of me, I will still be okay.

3. I Don't Have to Control Things

I will survive if things are different than what I want them to be. I can accept things the way they are, accept people the way they are, and accept myself the way I am. There is no reason to get upset if I can't change things to fit my idea of how they ought to be. There is no reason why I should have to like everything. Even if I don't like it, I can live with it.

4. I am Responsible for My Day

I am responsible for how I feel and what I do. Nobody can make me feel anything. If I have a **rotten**[1] day, I am the one who allows it to be that way. If I have a great day, I am the one who **deserves**[2] credit for being positive. It is not the responsibility of other people to change so that I can feel better. I am the one who is in charge of my life.

5. I Can Handle It When Things Go Wrong

I don't need to watch out for things to go wrong. Things usually go just fine, and when they don't, I can handle it. I don't have to waste my energy worrying. The sky won't fall in; things will be okay.

6. I am **Capable**[3]

I don't need someone else to take care of my problems. I am capable. I can take care of myself. I can make decisions for myself. I can think for myself. I don't have to depend on somebody else to take care of me.

7. I Can be **Flexible**[4]

There is more than one way to do something. More than one person has had good ideas that will work. There is no one and only "best" way. Everybody has ideas that are worthwhile. Some may make more sense to me than others, but everyone's ideas are worthwhile, and everyone has something worthwhile to contribute.

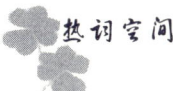

1. rotten ['rɔtn] *adj.* 腐烂的;堕落的
2. deserve [di'zə:v] *v.* 应受;值得
3. capable ['keipəbl] *adj.* 有能力的;能干的;有可能的
4. flexible ['fleksəbl] *adj.* 柔韧性;易曲的

金钱能买到幸福吗

佚名

金钱买得到幸福吗？买不到！但是，钱多一点，幸福是不是也会多些呢？我们很多人会咧嘴一笑，点点头。我们相信，财富的多少与精神愉悦之间有些关联。多数人会说：我们确实想成为富人。现在，美国大学生中有 3/4 的人认为，"经济的富足"是"非常重要"或"必不可少"。金钱的确重要。

富人更幸福吗？研究人员发现，在一些贫困国家里，相对的富足的确能使安康的可能性更大。我们需要食物、休息、庇护所和社会联系。

但是，生活中有这样一个事实，实在令人惊讶。在那些几乎每个人都能拥有生活必需品的国家里，财富的增长对幸福的影响并不大。收入和幸福之间的相互关系是"令人惊异的微小"，密歇根大学研究员罗纳德·英格利哈特在他的调查报告中是这样评述的——他曾对 16 个国家的 17 万人口做了调查。一旦人们的生活安逸了，增加了的物质财富所带来的幸福感则会逐渐降低。第二张馅饼永远没有第一张味道鲜美，或者，第二次 10 万美圆带来的兴奋感远不如第一次强烈。

甚至连彩票中奖者和《财富》杂志上选出的全美国最富有的前 100 人都表示，他们感受到的幸福只是比一般美国人稍微多一点点而已。发大财带来的只是暂时的快乐。但是，从长远来看，财富就像健康一样：完全缺失，会令苦难滋生，但拥有却不能保证幸福。幸福似乎并不是得到我们想要的东西，而是想要我们拥有的东西。

经济浪潮回升，我们的幸福感是否会随之上涨呢？今天，我们是否比 1940 年更幸福呢？那时候，2/5 的家庭还没有淋浴或浴盆；往炉子里添一块木头或煤炭就是取暖了;35%的家庭没有卫生间。

事实上,我们并没比以前更幸福。从1957年以来,美国人中,说自己"很幸福"的人数从35%降至32%。与此同时,离婚率是原来的两倍,青少年自杀率几乎是原来的3倍,犯罪率则高达原来的4倍(尽管最近有所降低),消极的人(特别是青少年)越来越多,超过了以往任何时候。

这种财富飞速增长,精神却不断委靡的状况,我称之为"美国矛盾"。我们拥有了大房子,家庭却破裂了;收入高了,精神却更低落;有了可靠的权利,却失去了礼貌;我们善于谋生,却往往不会营造生活;我们庆祝成功,又怀念目标;我们珍视自由,却又渴望交流。在这个物质充裕的时代,我们的精神却感到饥渴。

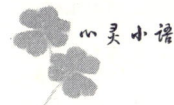

  人们的生活安逸后,物质财富增加所带来的幸福感反而会逐渐降低。因此可以断定,财富绝对不是幸福的真谛,它并不能买到真正的幸福,财富是必要的,但不是绝对的!真心真意的爱才是快乐和美好!

Does Money Buy Happiness

Anonymous

Does money buy happiness? Not! Ah, but would a little more money make us a little happier? Many of us **smirk**[1] and nod. There is, we believe, some connection between fiscal fitness and feeling fantastic. Most of us would say that, yes, we would like to be rich. Three in four American collegians now consider it "very important" or "essential" that they become "very well off financially". Money matters.

Well, are rich people happier? Researchers have found that in poor countries, being relatively well off does make for greater well-being. We need food, rest, shelter and social contact.

But a surprising fact of life is that in countries where nearly everyone can afford life's necessities, increasing affluence matters surprisingly little. The correlation between income and happiness is "surprisingly weak", observed University of Michigan researcher Ronald Inglehart in one 16-nation study of 170,000 people. Once comfortable, more money provides diminishing returns. The second piece of pie, or the second $100,000, never tastes as good as the first.

Even **lottery**[2] winners and the *Forbes*' 100 wealthiest Americans have expressed only slightly greater happiness than the average American. Making it big brings temporary joy. But in the long run wealth is like health: its utter absence can breed misery, but having it doesn't guarantee happiness. Happiness seems less a matter of getting what we want than of wanting what we have.

Has our happiness floated upward with the rising economic tide? Are we happier today than in 1940, when two out of five homes lacked a shower or tub? When heat often meant feeding wood or coal into a furnace? When 35 percent of homes had no toilet?

Actually, we are not. Since 1957, the number of Americans who say they are "very happy" has declined from 35 to 32 percent, Meanwhile, the divorce rate has doubled, the teen suicide rate has nearly tripled, the violent crime rate has nearly **quadrupled**[3] (even after the recent decline), and more people than ever (especially teens and young adults) are depressed.

I call this soaring wealth and shrinking spirit "the American paradox". More than ever, we have big houses and broken homes, high incomes and low **morale**[4], secured rights and diminished civility. We excel at making a living but often fail at making a life. We celebrate our prosperity but yearn for purpose. We cherish our freedoms but long for connection. In an age of plenty, we feel spiritual hunger.

热词空间

1. smirk [smə:k] v. 傻笑
2. lottery ['lɔtəri] n. 抽彩给奖法
3. quadruple ['kwɔdrupl] v. 成为四倍
4. morale [mɔ'ra:l] n. 士气；民心

我们在享受快乐吗

佚名

我们都被洗了脑!我们被灌输了这样的职业道德:"工作(和忍受)到生命的最后一刻,幸运的话,就直到退休。我们没有时间浪费在无聊的事情上。我们有体现自身价值的责任。我们一定要认真而努力地工作,在事业上进步,赚更多的钱,并把赚钱和事业进步看作生活的首要目标。"

我希望变更自己的人生计划。我知道,做自己感兴趣的事情,我会做得更好;做自己憎恶的事,我会做得一塌糊涂;在压力下工作通常会事倍功半。

我们可以改变生活中衡量某事是否该做的标准。我们需要扪心自问的不应是"它是否会赚大钱或能否让事业更上一层楼",而是"我对这感兴趣吗?这事有意思吗?我要大干一番吗?"

如果你不能肯定地回答这些问题,那么,这些很有可能就不是你该做的事情!

如果是诸如纳税、洗碗等你必须做的事情,解决的办法就是找别人代你做,你不喜欢做的事情自有人喜欢做。的确如此!举个例子来说,我并非世界上最棒的家庭主妇,我讨厌打扫卫生,擦地板和窗户等家务活,可偏偏有些人喜欢这种冥想性质的工作,并能在工作圆满完成后获得真正的满足。如果我雇人来做这些事,我则可以利用这些时间去做自己喜欢的事情来赚钱,这于我大有裨益。

人各有不同,不同的人适合做不同的事。某人喜欢做特定的某件事,这并不意味着你也必须要去喜欢。我所谓的"乐趣指数"可以用来帮助我们了解某一行为适合哪些人去做。判断一件事情是否该去做,不能只凭它能否带来物质利益和事业进步等经验主义,而应看此事是否能给我们带来乐趣并使我们获得满足感。你的工作带给你自豪感和满足感了吗?你是在执行"应该"指令还是依照"想做"的意愿呢?

然而，这种程式是异常强大的。我发现，勉强自己做事的结果就是能拖则拖、没完没了。你留意过吗？做自己不喜欢的事情似乎总也做不完。反之，则如俗语所云："乐在其中，浑然不知所谓何日。"

我们要反对旧的程式，并相信"乐趣指数"是一个流动工程。每个小的进步同时也是一个大的飞跃。每一步都会淡化你对生活的不满情绪，强化你的自爱、自我认同和自尊感，让你更易感知生活中的乐趣。

不论何时，你都不能忽视这种内在激励，否则，你便会日益陷入自厌与自责的泥潭，再次感到消沉没落。每一次的失望都会强化心中的那个信念：别人的愿望比自己的更加重要。于是，你内在的欲求便会再次被压抑到最低位置。

但是，这就是你的生活！为何要让他人指示你"应该"怎样生活呢？问问你自己，你想怎样规划自己的人生！聆听内心的声音，它会告诉你什么会真正充实和满足你。要知道，你才是自己生活的主宰者！毕竟，这是你的生活，不是吗？

心灵小语

生活是属于自己的，快乐也是属于自己的，不要让别人来设计你的生活，不要让别人来告诉你该做什么、不该做什么，那样你就会失去自我的选择，失去其实本该属于你的快乐。学会控制自己的生活，掌握自己的幸福！

Are We Having Fun Yet

Anonymous

We've all been brainwashed! We were all taught the work ethic! "Work (and suffer) till you die, or if you're lucky retire. We don't have time to waste on frivolities. We have responsibilities to fulfill. We have to be serious, work hard, rise in our career, make lots of money, and make earning money and advancing in our career a priority."

I wish to change that programming in my life. I know that when I do the things I enjoy doing, things work out better for me. I know that when I do something against my will, against my heart, it doesn't work out well. I know that stressing myself out to try to get a job done usually takes twice as long as taking time out and doing that same task at some other time in a relaxed manner.

We can change the criteria by which we decide what to do in our lives. Instead of "Will it bring in lots of money or advance my career", we need to ask ourselves, "Will I enjoy doing this? Will this be fun? Am I looking forward to getting started on this?"

If you can't answer "yes" to these questions, then quite possibly this is not the task for you!

If it is something that must be done, i.e. taxes, dishes, etc., the solution is to find someone else to do them for you. There are some people who will enjoy and love to do what you prefer not to do. Really! For example, I am not the world's best housekeeper. I do not really enjoy cleaning, washing floors, windows, etc. Yet there are some people who enjoy the meditative aspect of this work and who really get satisfaction from a job well done. It is to my benefit to pay someone to do this work so I can take that time earning money doing things that I enjoy.

We are all very different and different things appeal to each one of us. Just because someone else enjoys a particular thing does not mean that you must. We can trust what I call the "fun index" to assist us in knowing if a particular action is the one for us. We can break away from the rule of thumb that judges things by whether they bring money or career advancement. We can change that to making our decisions based on whether an action will bring us pleasure and personal satisfaction. Does the work you do leave you feeling proud and pleased with yourself? Are you following the voice of "shoulds" or the one of "want to"?

Yet, the programming is strong. I find myself struggling over a task and it ends up dragging itself out. Have you noticed that the things that you dislike doing are the ones that seem to take forever to get done? As for the opposite viewpoint, well as the saying goes, "Time flies when you're having fun!"

Learning to go against that old programming and trusting the "fun index" is an ongoing project. Every small step is, at the same time, a big leap. Each step will move you away from dissatisfaction with your life and closer to self-love, self-acceptance, self-esteem and joy in your everyday existence.

Anytime you ignore that inner prompting, you accumulate self-loathing and disappointment in your being. Your inner child once again feels letdown and unimportant. Each letdown reinforce the inner child's belief that everybody else's wishes are more important than its own. Once again its desires are relegated to the lowest priority on the list.

Yet, it's YOUR life! Why let someone else dictate how you "should" live it? Ask yourself what steps YOU want to take! Listen to the voice within which will tell you what would really make you feel fulfilled and satisfied. YOU ARE the boss of your life! After all, it's yours, isn't it?

幸福

佚名

很多人认为,拥有财富与声望之时,便是幸福到来之际。我得告诉你,事实并非如此。这个世界,富有却痛苦得如同生活在地狱的人比比皆是。关于电影明星自杀或吸毒致死的报道,我们读过无数。毫无疑问,金钱并非是解决全部问题的唯一办法。

不义之财无法带来幸福。彩票中奖不能带来幸福。赌博所得不可能带来幸福。在我看来,幸福的秘诀在于工作卓有成就,在于对他人的幸福有所贡献,在于诚实致富。凭运气或靠欺骗得来的钱财是不义之财。利用他人或伤害他人得来的钱财,你不会乐于接受,你会觉得自己自私卑鄙。

建立在诚实正直、卓有成效的工作、贡献和自尊的基础上的幸福才会长久。幸福不是终点,而是一个过程。这个过程需要连续不断的诚实正直、卓有成效地工作。它让你真正有益于他人,让你意识到自身的价值。正如韦恩博士所说:"没有通向幸福的路,幸福本身就是路。""有朝一日,我实现了自己的目标,有车有房,拥有自己的事业,那么我就会幸福"——这种说法毫无意义。生活不会是这样的。若是等到某些东西的出现,依赖外部环境的改变,你才感到幸福,那你永远若有所失,总会错过某些东西。

心灵小语

千百年来,许多人的一生都是在寻找幸福中度过的,或许直到生命终结时,才会想到,原来幸福就在我们身边,只是我们没有尽情享受。把握身边的每一秒,抓住属于自己的幸福,不要将注意力放在"等待"上,这样只会让自己更累,更感到幸福的遥远!

Happiness

Anonymous

Many people think that when they become rich and successful, happiness will naturally follow. Let me tell you that nothing is further from the truth. The world is full of very rich people who are as miserable as if they were living in hell. We have read stories about movie stars who committed suicide or died from drugs. Quite clearly, money is not the only answer to all problems.

Wealth obtained through dishonest means does not bring happiness. Lottery winnings do not bring happiness. Gamble winnings do not bring happiness. To my mind, the secret to happiness lies in your successful work, in your contribution towards others' happiness and in your wealth you have earned through your own honest effort. If you obtain wealth through luck or dishonest means, you will know that it is ill earned money. If you get your money by taking advantage of others or by hurting others, you will not be happy with it. You will think you are a base person.

Long-term happiness is based on honesty, productive work, contribution, and self-esteem. Happiness is not an end; it is a process. It is a continuous process of honest, productive work which makes a real contribution to others and makes you feel you are a useful, worthy person. As Dr. Wayne wrote, "There is no way to happiness. Happiness is the way." There is no use saying "Some day when I achieve these goals, when I get a car, build a house and own my own business, then I will be really happy". Life just does not work that way. If you wait for certain things to happen and depend on external circumstances of life to make you happy, you will always feel unfulfilled. There will always be something missing.

选择乐观

佚名

　　如果你预料某事会很糟糕,那么它很可能真会这样。悲观的想法一般都能实现。但反过来,这个原理也同样成立。如果你料想会好运连连,通常也会这样!乐观和成功之间似乎有一种天然的因果关系。

　　乐观和悲观都是强大的力量,我们塑造和展望未来,都必须从中做出选择。每个人的生命中都有太多的幸运或灾难:充满着忧伤和快乐、无限的喜悦和痛苦——不论我们是悲观还是乐观,都有充分的理由。我们可以选择哭或笑,祝福或诅咒。这是我们的决定:选择用什么样的眼光来看待人生? 是在希望中昂首阔步,还是在绝望中低头长叹?

　　我喜欢展望未来。我选择注意积极面,忽视消极面。我是乐观主义者,更多的是因为我的选择,而非天性。当然,我知道,生命中总存在着悲伤。现在,我已经70多岁了,经历过太多灾难。但是,当一切尘埃落定,我发现生命中的美好远多于丑恶。

　　乐观的态度并非奢侈品,而是一种必需。你看待生活的方式决定了你如何去感受,去表现,以及你与他人如何相处。相反,消极的思想、态度和预想也决定了这些,它们成为一种能自我实现的预言。悲观会制造一种阴沉的生活,没有人愿意活在其中。

　　几年前,我开车去一个加油站加油。那天天气很晴朗,我心情很好。当我进站付油费时,服务员对我说:"你感觉怎么样啊?"这个问题有些莫名其妙,但我感觉很好,也这样跟他说了。"你脸色不大好,"他说。我十分惊讶,于是,我告诉他,我确实感觉不错,但已不在信心十足了。他毫不犹豫地继续说我脸色如何不好,连皮肤都发黄了。

美丽英文
Beautiful English

我心神不宁地离开加油站,开了一个街区后,我把车停在路边,照着镜子看看自己的脸。我怎么了?是不是得了黄疸病了?一切都正常吗?回到家时,我开始想吐了,我的肝脏是不是出了问题?我不会染上什么怪病了吧?

我再次去那个加油站时,又感觉不错了,也明白了究竟是怎么一回事。这个地方最近涂了一种明亮、胆汁质的黄色油漆,灯光反射在墙壁上,让里面的人看起来像是得了肝炎。我想,不知道有多少人也有过类似的经历呢。我的心情却因为与一个完全陌生的人短暂的交谈,整整改变了一天。他告诉我,我看起来像生病了,而后不久,我真的感觉不舒服。这个消极的观点,深刻地影响了我的感受和行为。

唯一比消极更具力量的是一个积极的肯定,一个乐观和希望的言词。最令我欣慰的是,我是在一个有着乐观主义光荣传统的国度里成长的。当整体文化积极向上时,再难以置信的事也能完成。当世界看起来充满希望,人们就会在这个积极的场所,努力向上并获得成功。

乐观并不需要变得幼稚,我们可以在成为乐观者的同时,仍意识到有问题存在,有些甚至难以解决。但是,乐观使解决问题的态度有所不同!乐观会使我们把注意力从消极转向积极的、建设性的思考上。如果你是一个乐观者,会更关心问题的解决而不是毫无价值地怨天尤人。事实上,如果没有乐观主义精神,一些现存的巨大问题,如贫穷,就毫无希望解决。它需要一个梦想家——一个拥有绝对乐观、矢志不移、坚定信念的人——来解决这个巨大的问题。乐观,或是悲观,在于你的选择。

心灵小语

积极、乐观的生活态度可以帮助我们更好的生活,更真切地体会生活的真谛,对于乐观者,痛苦可以变成快乐,不益可以变成有益。如果一个人是悲观的,那他的生活必定是灰暗的!生命苦短,就更要乐观地对待生活,享受它赐予我们的一切。

Choose Optimism

Anonymous

If you expect something to turn out badly, it probably will. Pessimism is seldom disappointed. But the same principle also works in reverse. If you expect good things to happen, they usually do! There seems to be a natural cause-and-effect relationship between optimism and success.

Optimism and pessimism are both powerful forces, and each of us must choose which we want to shape our outlook and our expectations. There is enough good and bad in everyone's life —ample sorrow and happiness, sufficient joy and pain—to find a rational basis for either optimism or pessimism. We can choose to laugh or cry, bless or curse. It's our decision: From which perspective do we want to view life? Will we look up in hope or down in despair?

I believe in the upward look. I choose to highlight the positive and slip right over the negative. I am an optimist by choice as much as by nature. Sure, I know that sorrow exists. I am in my 70s now, and I've lived through more than one crisis. But when all is said and done, I find that the good in life far outweighs the bad.

An optimistic attitude is not a luxury; it's a necessity. The way you look at life will determine how you feel, how you perform, and how well you will get along with other people. Conversely, negative thoughts, attitudes, and expectations feed on themselves; they become a self-fulfilling prophecy. Pessimism creates a dismal place where no one wants to live.

Years ago, I drove into a service station to get some gas. It was a beautiful day, and I was feeling great. As I walked into the station to pay for the gas, the attendant said to me, "How do you feel?" That seemed like an odd question, but I felt fine and told him so. "You don't look well," he replied. This took me completely by surprise. A little less confidently, I told him that I had never felt better. Without hesitation, he continued to tell me how bad I looked and that my skin appeared yellow.

By the time I left the service station, I was feeling a little uneasy. About a block away, I pulled over to the side of the road to look at my face in the mirror. How did I feel? Was I jaundiced ? Was everything all right? By the time I got home, I was beginning to feel a little queasy. Did I have a bad liver? Had I picked up some rare disease?

The next time I went into that gas station, feeling fine again, I figured out what had happened. The place had recently been painted a bright, bilious yellow, and the light reflecting off the walls made everyone inside look as though they had hepatitis! I wondered how many other folks had reacted the way I did. I had let one short conversation with a total stranger change my attitude for an entire day. He told me I looked sick, and before long, I was actually feeling sick. That single negative observation had a profound effect on the way I felt and acted.

The only thing more powerful than negativism is a positive affirmation, a word of optimism and hope. One of the things I am most thankful for is the fact that I have grown up in a nation with a grand tradition of optimism. When a whole culture adopts an upward look, incredible things can be accomplished. When the world is seen as a hopeful, positive place, people are empowered to attempt and to achieve.

Optimism doesn't need to be naive. We can be an optimist and still recognize that problems exist and that some of them are not dealt with easily. But what a difference optimism makes in the attitude of the problem solver! Optimism diverts our attention away from negativism and channels it into positive, constructive thinking. When you're an optimist, you're more concerned with problem-solving than with useless carping about issues. In fact, without optimism, issues as big and ongoing as poverty have no hope of solution. It takes a dreamer—someone with hopelessly optimistic ideas, great persistence, and unlimited confidence—to tackle a problem that big. It's your choice.

快乐真言

佚名

我以前并不是一个非常快乐的孩子,像大多数十几岁的孩子一样,我总是沉浸在自己的烦恼中。但是,有一天,我豁然开朗,谁都有可能不快乐,因为那不需要任何勇气或努力。而快乐,却存在真正的挑战,需要不断地付出努力。

也许很多人都未曾听说过,快乐也要付出努力。我们以为这种感受只是一些美好事物所产生的必然结果,纯粹是一种偶然,我们很少或者说根本无法控制。

然而,事实刚好相反:在很大程度上,我们自己控制着快乐。它是一场需要发起的战斗,而不是那种守株待兔的感觉。

要让生活更加快乐,我们必须扫除这些绊脚石,其中三个是:

与他人攀比

大多数人都喜欢与自认为比自己快乐的人比较——一个亲戚,熟人,或者通常是我们不甚了解的人。我曾经遇到一个年轻人,他的巨大成功和快乐让我羡慕不已。他说他非常爱自己漂亮的妻子和女儿们,也为能在自己喜欢的城市做一个电台脱口秀节目主持人而感到高兴。我记得当时自己以为他是那些为数不多的幸运儿之一,一切都那么轻而易举。

然后我们谈到了因特网,他告诉我,他感激它的存在,因为从网上能查到大量硬化症的信息——他的妻子一直承受着这种可怕疾病的折磨。我竟愚蠢地认为他的生活没有丝毫不快。

幻想完美

几乎每个人都对自己的生活有一番设想。可问题是,人们的工作、配偶和孩子很少能达到理想的境地。

就拿我的亲身经历来说:我的家族中以前从未有人离过婚,我也认为结婚是一辈子的事。所以,当我和妻子在儿子出生三年后离婚时,觉得整个世界都崩塌了,我认定自己是一个失败者。

后来,我向再婚的妻子弗兰倾诉苦楚:我认为自己的家庭生活已经失败,而这样感觉一直无法摆脱。她问我,我们现在的家庭(包括她和前夫的女儿,我的儿子)有什么问题吗？我必须承认，除了只有一半的时间与儿子相处，令我感到痛苦外（我和前妻分担监护权），我们的家庭生活非常美满幸福。

"那么，为什么你不因此而庆幸呢？"她问道。

我正决定这样做，但首先我必须清除想象中的"完美家庭"。

"缺失的砖块"综合征

紧盯着某物微乎其微的瑕疵，会极大地破坏幸福，就像抬头看天花板，注意力只集中在缺失一块瓷砖的地方。正如一个秃顶的人告诉我，"无论何时走进一个房间，我看到的全是头发。"

我花了几年时间研究快乐，得出的最重要的结论之一是：人们感受快乐的程度，与他们的生活条件并无太大关联。只要想想，这个结论便显而易见了。我们都知道，一些人的生活相对安逸，却并不快乐。我们也知道，有些人遭受了巨大的痛苦，却仍旧很开心。

第一个秘诀是感恩的心。所有快乐的人都满怀感激，而不知感恩的人则感受不到快乐。我们以为不快乐的人才会一味地抱怨，但事实上，正是抱怨使人们变得不快乐。

第二个秘诀是认识到快乐是一种其他事情的副产品。快乐最主要的来源，是能让生活更有意义的一切追求——从研究昆虫到打棒球。我们拥有更多的激情，就会感受更多的快乐。

最后，相信某种永恒会超越我们，我们的存在有更伟大的意义，这些会帮助我们享受更多快乐。我们需要精神上或宗教上的信仰，或是一种生活的哲理。你的人生哲学应该包括这个公认的真理：在任何情况下，如果你都选择发现事实的积极面，那你会感到快乐；如果你选择关注消极面，你就会痛苦。快乐本身，很大程度上，取决于你所做的决定。

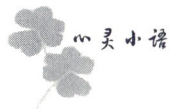

在任何情况下，如果你都选择发现事物的积极面，那你会感到快乐；如果你选择关注消极面，你就会痛苦。因为快乐本身，很大程度上，取决于你所做的决定。

A Simple Truth about Happiness

Anonymous

I was not a particularly happy child, and like most teenagers, I reveled in my angst. One day, however, it occurred to me that I was taking the easy way out. Anyone could be unhappy; it took no courage or effort. True challenge lay in struggling to be happy.

The notion that we have to work at happiness comes as news to many people. We assume it's a feeling that comes as a result of good things that just happen to us, things over which we have little or no control.

But the opposite is true: happiness is largely under our control. It is a battle to be waged and not a feeling to be awaited.

To achieve a happier life, it's necessary to overcome some stumbling blocks, three of which are:

Comparison with Others

Most of us compare ourselves with anyone we think is happier—a relative, an acquaintance or, often, someone we barely know. I once met a young man who struck me as particularly successful and happy. He spoke of his love for his beautiful wife and their daughters, and of his joy at being a radio talk-show host in a city he loved. I remember thinking he was one of those lucky few for whom everything goes effortlessly right.

Then we started talking about the Internet. He blessed its existence, he told me, because he could look up information on multiple sclerosis—the terrible disease afflicting his wife. I felt like a fool for assuming nothing unhappy existed in his life.

Images of Perfection

Almost any of us have images of how life should be. The problem, of course, is that only rarely do people's jobs, spouses and children live up to these imagined ideals.

Here's a personal example: No one in my family had ever divorced. I assumed that marriage was for life. So when my wife and I divorced three years after the birth of our son, my world caved in. I was a failure in my own eyes.

I later remarried but confided to my wife, Fran that I couldn't shake the feeling that my family life had failed. She asked me what was wrong with our family now (which included her daughter from a previous marriage and my son). I had to admit that, aside from the pain of being with my son only half the time (my ex-wife and I shared custody), our family life was wonderful.

"Then why don't you celebrate it?" she asked.

That's what I decided to do. But first I had to get rid of the image of a "perfect" family.

"Missing Tile" Syndrome

One effective way of sabotaging happiness is to look at something and be fixated on even the smallest flaw. It's like looking up at a filed ceiling and concentrating on the space where one tile is missing. As a bald man told me, "Whenever I enter a room, all I see is hair."

I've spent years studying happiness, and one of the most significant conclusions I've drawn is this: there is little correlation between the circumstances of people's lives and how happy they are. A moment's reflection should make this obvious. We all know people who have had a relatively easy life yet are essentially unhappy. And we know people who have suffered a great deal but generally remain happy.

The first secret is gratitude. All happy people are grateful. Ungrateful people cannot be happy. We tend to think that being unhappy leads people to complain, but it's truer to say that complaining leads to people becoming unhappy.

The second secret is realizing that happiness is a by-product of something else. The most obvious sources are those pursuits that give our lives purpose—anything from studying insects to playing baseball. The more passions we have, the more happiness we're likely to experience.

Finally, the belief that something permanent transcends us and that our existence has some larger meaning can help us be happier. We need a spiritual or religious faith, or a philosophy of life. Your philosophy should encompass this truism: if you choose to find the positive in virtually every situation, you will be blessed, and if you choose to find the awful, you will be cursed. As with happiness itself, this is largely your decision to make.

快乐法则

佚名

记住如下五条简单的快乐法则：
1. 让心灵从憎恨中解脱；
2. 让情绪从焦虑中解脱；
3. 简单地生活；
4. 更多地付出；
5. 更少地期待。

没有人能回到过去，重新开始，但谁都可以从现在开始，开创一个崭新的未来。

上帝并未承诺我们没有痛苦的日子，没有悲伤的欢笑，没有雨天的阳光，但是他给予了我们生活的力量，安慰着我们痛苦的心灵，也照亮了我们前行的方向。

失望就像人生道路上的山丘，它们使你前行的脚步迟缓，但是，一旦越过它们，你便踏上了坦途。

不要在山丘上停留太久。继续前进！

当你为得不到渴求的东西而沮丧时，请坚持你的渴求，并快乐地等待，因为上帝正在考虑让更好的事降临到你头上。

不论发生什么事，不管是好是坏，思考它的意义吧。生活的目的是教会你如何开心更多、伤心更少。

你不能强求他人爱上你，你只能力求做一个值得别人爱的人，剩下就看他人如何认可你的价值了。

权衡爱的标准就是毫无条件地去爱。

生活中,遇到你爱的并且爱你的人并不容易,因而,一旦遇到了,请一定要珍惜,这样的机会不可能有第二次。

为你所爱的人放弃自己的骄傲要比为了骄傲而失去你所爱的人好得多。

我们花太多的时间去寻找真爱,去挑剔爱人的缺点。事实上,我们应全身心地为爱付出。

当你真正在乎一个人时,你就不会对他吹毛求疵,不会找原因,也不会挑他的过错。相反,你会原谅他的过错,接受他的缺点,忽略他的借口。

不要与老朋友断绝往来,没有人能够替代他。要知道,友谊如酒,越久越醇。

快乐也是有法则的,你知道吗?读了上面的文章你就可获得这样一个快乐锦囊,按上面的指示做,你就会发现一些平时并不注意的细节,并发掘出其中的幸福与快乐,在幸福中品味情感,在快乐中享受生活!

Five Simple Rules

Anonymous

Remember the five simple rules to be happy:
1. Free your heart from **hatred**[1];
2. Free your mind from worries;
3. Live simply
4. Give more;
5. Expect less.

No one can go back and make a brand new start. Anyone can start from now and make a brand new ending.

God didn't promise days without pain, laughter without sorrow, sun without rain, but He did promise strength for the day, comfort for the tears and light for the way.

Disappointments[2] are like road **humps**[3], they slow you down a bit but you enjoy the smooth road afterwards.

Don't stay on the humps too long. Move on!

When you feel down because you didn't get what you wanted, just sit tight and be happy because God is thinking of something better to give you.

When something happens to you, good or bad, consider what it means. There's a purpose to life's events, to teach you how to laugh more or not to cry too hard.

You can't make someone love you, all you can do is being someone who can be loved, and the rest is up to the person to realize your worth.

The measure of love is when you love without measure.

In life there are very rare chances that you'll meet the person you love and loves you in return. So once you have it don't ever let go, the chance might never come your way again.

It's better to lose your pride to the one you love than to lose the one you love because of pride.

We spend too much time looking for the right person to love or finding fault with those we already love, when instead we should be perfecting the love we give.

When you truly care for someone, you don't look for faults, you don't look for answers, and you don't look for mistakes. Instead, you forgive the mistakes, you accept the faults, and you overlook the excuses.

Never **abandon**[4] an old friend. You will never find one who can take his place. Friendship is like wine, it gets better as it grows older.

热词空间

1. hatred ['heitrid] n. 憎恨;敌意;仇恨
2. disappointment [ˌdisəˈpɔintmənt] n. 失望
3. hump [hʌmp] n. 驼峰;驼背;峰丘
4. abandon [əˈbændən] v. 放弃;遗弃;放任;狂热

幸福是一种感觉

佚名

有一天在杂货店,我和一个朋友排队购物时,我不断地向她诉说我的孩子们是多么懒惰。那天清晨,我上完晚班回家,房间又像多数时候那样,乱作一团。

"我觉得,如今的孩子总是一味索取,我为他们竭尽全力,可他们甚至都不能帮我保持房间整洁。就算我不烦,其他女人看到我那又脏又乱的房间,也会指责我。"

"你知道自己多幸福吗?"我们身后的一个女人说道,"我非常希望回到家后,能看到房子里混乱不堪。地毯弄脏了,或者到处是碟子、成堆的脏衣服、混杂的袜子,我都不介意,甚至别人要说我的房子有多脏,我也不在乎。事实上,我就喜欢那样。只要能再和我的孩子们在一起,能拥抱、亲吻并告诉他们,我是多么爱他们,我就非常愿意踢开脚边的杂物,在混乱的房子里穿行。你知道吗?在一次车祸中,我的两个孩子都遇难了,现在只剩下我和丈夫,我的房子总是很干净,衣服堆放整洁,碟子也摆放妥当。

"墙壁上没有手指印,莫名其妙的污点也不会出现在地毯上。房子里没有吵闹声,没有砰的关门声,没有笑声,也听不到有人说'我爱你,妈妈'。所以,要知道,你是多么幸福啊!此刻你所反感的一切正是我渴望得到的。我多么希望能抱着自己的孩子,擦干他们的眼泪,分享他们的梦想,或者只是看着他们玩耍。如果我还有孩子,房子再乱我也不在乎,只要拥有他们,我就开心了。"

现在,如果你进了我的房子,看到一片混乱。你觉得多糟糕我都无所谓,因为我感到非常幸福。

心灵小语

有时候,麻烦也是一种幸福,就看我们以一个怎样的角度来看待它。当你的孩子经常吵闹的时候,你会觉得他们很烦;当你的孩子离你而去了,你就会感到原来孩子的吵闹也是一种幸福。因为幸福是一种感觉。

Blessed

Anonymous

A friend and I were standing in line at the grocery store the other day, and I was telling her how lazy my children were. I had come in from work that morning, and like most times, my house was wrecked.

"I believe children nowadays are just out for what they can get. I bend over backwards for them, and they can't even help keep our house clean. It wouldn't bother me so, but it's the woman who looks bad if the house is a mess."

"Do you know how blessed you are?" A woman behind us asked. "I would love to go home and find my house a mess. I wouldn't mind my carpet being ruined or the dishes left everywhere. I wouldn't mind the dirty clothes being piled high or the many socks to match. I wouldn't even mind anyone talking about my dirty home. Matter of fact, I would love it. I would dearly love to kick my way through the house just to get to my kids and be able to hug them, kiss them and tell them how much I love them. You see, my two children were killed in an auto accident and now it's just my husband and me. My house stays clean, my clothes stay put up, the dishes are done.

"There are no fingerprints on my walls, no mysterious spots on my carpets. There are no sounds of arguing, no slamming doors, no laughter, no I love you Mom. So you see, you are very blessed. What I would give to be going through what you are right now. How I would love to be able to hold my kids, wipe away their tears, share their dreams. Just to watch them play. If I had my children, I wouldn't care how my house looked. I would be happy just to have them."

Now if you come into my house and see a big old mess, you can think bad thoughts if you want, but I feel greatly blessed.

幸福箴言

佚名

虽然有时我给读者一种悲观的错觉,但我从来不是一个本质悲观的人。我更倾向于乐观,因为我非常严肃地看待生命。

悲观是浪费精力的情绪——是用以惩罚那些不知如何生活之人的。

行动才有幸福,每一股力量都是为了行动。

我始终觉得,无所事事比努力工作要痛苦得多。

快乐和热情是所有美德中最宝贵的。

逆境比顺境更能激发热情。

满足源于对周围环境的一种内在优越感。

我们常误认为展望未来意味着对未来的忧虑。满怀憧憬与愁眉紧锁一样容易。

几乎世上所有的罪恶和不幸都源于自私。我们很清楚这点,却仍执迷不悟地自私。

不能带来快乐的荣誉只能是一种遗憾。

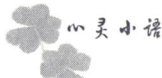
心灵小语

悲观,只会让我们的生活白白流逝,只会让身边的快乐悄悄溜走。悲观是浪费精力的情绪——是用以惩罚那些不知如何生活之人的。行动才是幸福,每一股力量都是为了行动。快乐的生活才是我们的选择,纵情欢笑、奔跑、跳跃,让我们在这片蔚蓝的天空下尽情快乐吧!

On Happiness

Anonymous

I have never been basically **pessimistic**[1], although I have appeared so to some readers.

I have taken life so seriously as to be disposed to optimism.

Pessimism is a waste of force—the penalty of one who doesn't know how to live.

Happiness is in action, and every power is intended for action.

I have always found that it's more painful to do nothing than something.

Of all the **virtues**[2], cheerfulness and enthusiasm are the most profitable.

Enthusiasm[3] flourishes more often in adversity than it does in prosperity.

Contentment grows out of an inward superiority to our surroundings.

We fall into the mistake of supposing that to look forward must mean to look anxiously forward. It is just as easy to look forward with hope as with sadness.

The source of nearly all the evil and unhappiness of this world is selfishness. We know it; but we still keep on being selfish.

Fame without happiness is but a sorry at best.

1. pessimistic [ˌpesiˈmistik] *adj.* 悲观的;厌世的
2. virtue [ˈvəːtjuː] *n.* 德行;美德;贞操;优点
3. enthusiasm [inˈθjuːziæzəm] *n.* 狂热;热心;积极性

请喝杯茶

佚名

"**请**喝杯茶。"此时,我真想这样邀请你。每当与朋友一道喝茶闲聊时,我常思绪万千,并极力想把朋友的言辞、眼神和微笑一一典藏,唯恐曲终人散,再无相聚之时。我喜欢茶道里的"一生一会"之说,它意味着我们应该珍惜每一次与朋友品茶的机会,因为这样的机会只有一次,一旦错过,便不可复得。

想想,对我们来说,这样相聚的机会是多么难得,多么深刻和美好啊。人们常说,人生无常,命运多舛。正因如此,人人都追寻幸福和快乐。然而,幸福何在?幸福之一在于与密友重逢。由此看来,我们只有一路奔波,辛苦劳累,历经无数坎坷,无数磨砺后,才能再聚首。但是,使心灵振颤的一聚却成不惑之年的专利;这一聚的欢欣温暖着彼此的内心,成为一切喜怒哀乐的完美绽放;这相聚时刻的沉默就是饱含深意或空洞黯然的言辞的极大合成。啊,请细细品味这杯茶吧,它是浓缩天地灵气的茶树精华。

其实,我们是勇敢新世界的命运宠儿,它赐予我们四年相聚相知的时光。并且,即使彼此珍视关爱,也终将各赴前程,甚至永无相聚之日。明白这些,待分飞之时,纵使无缘再聚,也了无遗憾。或许,这即是所谓的"一生一会"吧,不是吗?

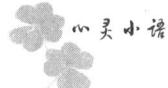

"请喝杯茶",希望亲爱的朋友停一停繁忙的脚步,大家一起分享这闲适、恬静的一刻,将这难得的一刻永存心中。品一口茶,将生活的烦忧一起冲淡,将内心的恼怒一起浇灭。朋友,所有的情感与不舍,尽在这小小的茶杯中,不管未来怎样,请对你的朋友们说一句,"请喝杯茶!"

A Cup of Tea

Anonymous

"Please have a cup of tea," I wish I could invite you at the moment.

You know, when chat over a cup of tea with friends, I often imagine boundless and try to collect in mind all words, expression in eyes and smile of friends as though the meeting will never return after saying goodbye. On tea ceremony, I love the parlance "a meeting in a lifetime" which seemly means that one should feel grateful for every time with friends to drink tea together because it might allow no what-ifs, and there would be no going back to the beginning.

As you can see, how rare, how grave and how nice the only meeting is to us! Many people often think that life is capricious and fate is hard, so everyone is pursuing happiness and joyfulness. Where is joyful? One is to meet bosom friends again. Judging from this, how many roads must we run and toil down with hardships and full of frustrations before the meeting call us together? Yet, the meeting that touch our hearts become the story of our forty; the smiling that warm our hearts become the flower of our pleasure, angry, sorrow and joy; the silence that inspire our hearts become the accomplishment of all our words significant or vaguely conscious. Ah, here is just a cup of tea and please enjoy it carefully because it has drawn the essence of tea trees to be created by the sun and the earth.

To be honest, we are fortune's favorite of the brave new world, which gave us a meeting lasting whole four years and made us knowing each other well. What's more, we would still be perfectly content without bit regret when we had to go each of our own ways, even we could never meet again if highly care and blessing, each in our minds, crystallized. Probably, this is a catch in a lifetime, is not it?

步行的乐趣

佚名

散步能唤醒我们的感官。散步时对这个世界的所见所闻所感,是乘车时所不曾有的。不管你搭乘什么交通工具,运动的是车,而不是我们自身。我们受车内特定环境所限,一旦适应了这种环境——主要侧重于是否舒适——就失去了自己的知觉,或睡觉或翻开杂志昏沉沉地打盹。

当我们散步时,周围的环境每一时刻都发生着变化,我们的感知也随之不断地转换。在城市街区的每一个拐角和乡村道路的每一个拐弯处,总有某种新鲜事物吸引我们的眼球和我们的听觉与嗅觉。即使我们每天走的是同一条人行路,每天也都会有所不同,每一周、每一季也会有所变化。

不仅是在乡村,其他各地也都如此。在纽约,有一群行政人员每天早上相遇,他们都是从家步行到办公室,途经古旧的褐色石头铺成的寂静街道,那是这座城市中最古老的街区之一。然后经过布鲁克林大桥,桥孔像大教堂拱顶一样,支撑着巨缆织成的桥板,然后走进峡谷般的金融区,那里两侧是巍然屹立的摩天大楼。

他们在每天经过的路上看到、听到、也闻到了纽约在明朗晴空和阴云密布的天空下的四季更迭。只有在天气极度恶劣、寒冷和狂风暴雨之时,他们才会畏惧前行。他们穿着应季的衣服,欢快地行走在春雨中、绵绵的秋雨中、夏日清晨的阳光下或冬日细软的飘雪中。河水流经他们脚下,或郁郁寡欢,或汩汩流淌。拖船突突地开过,用力地推着或拉着满载货物的驳船。在浓雾迷茫的清晨,雾号有时大声鸣响,有时呜咽呻吟。久富盛名的曼哈顿岛低垂的轮廓在地平线上方的天空升起,在阳光下闪烁,飘浮在雾霭里,那背景天幕变化万端,从不曾重复。

步行有助于排遣压力与不快。步行去上班,用一颗平静的心来欣赏美景,忘记工作的紧张与生活的烦忧,这一刻,我们就与自然同在,享受微风拂面,鸟儿高歌,吸吮这清新的空气,尽情享受生活的另一面!

The Pleasure of Walking

Anonymous

Walking gives us back our senses. We see, hear, smell the world as we never can when we ride. No matter what vehicle, it is the vehicle that is moving, not ourselves. We are trapped inside its fixed environment, and once we have taken in its sensory aspects—mainly in terms of comfort or discomfort—we turn off our perceptions and either go to sleep or open a magazine and begin dozing in and out.

But when we walk, the environment changes every moment and our senses are continuously being alerted. Around each corner of a city block, around each bend in a country road, there is something new to greet the eyes, the ears, the nose. Even the same walk, the one we may take every day, is never the same from one day to another, from one week and season to another.

This is true not only in the country, but everywhere else. In New York City, a group of executives who meet every weekday morning walk from their homes to their offices. Their way takes them through quiet streets of old brownstones, one of the oldest neighborhoods in the city, then up and over the Brooklyn Bridge with its cathedral arches supporting the web-like drapery of cables, then down into the tight skyscraper canyons of the financial district.

On their daily route they see, hear, smell the city in all its seasonal changes, under bright and cloudy skies. Only the most inclement weather stops them—suitably dressed, they can walk with pleasure in spring rains, autumn drizzles, the sunlight of a summer morning or a soft winter snowfall. The river waters roll by below their feet, sullen or sparkling. Tugboats chug past, shoving and hauling their variously laden barges; on a shrouded morning, foghorns hoot and moan. The famous skyline of lower Manhattan rises before them, glittering in sun, afloat in mist, against a backdrop of sky never twice the same.

幸福就在我们身边

佚名

生活就像一条被鲜花、蝴蝶和鲜果簇拥的曲折小径,可我们大多数人都费时费力地去僻远处寻找快乐,却偏偏不愿享受近在眼前的幸福。

我们都期望得到那只"金罐子",那里承载着全部持久的幸福,我们想用这些去充实自己的生活,却忽视了那些看似无益于实现远大抱负或不能使成功一蹴而就之事。

幸福就在我们身边,只是它总是一点一滴地出现。只要我们收集每一个颗粒,不久便会集满一篮。

此刻,有哪些点滴的幸福围绕在我的周围呢?

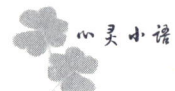
心灵小语

对我们来说,幸福是复杂多样的,但获得幸福的方式却相同。幸福不是发生在我们周围的事——而是我们如何去看待周围发生的事。幸福并非是乞求我们未得到的,而是享受我们此刻所有的一切。只要我们有"感受快乐的能力",那么我们都会生活得很幸福。

Happiness Is All Around Us

Anonymous

Life is like a winding path surrounded by flowers, **butterflies**[1], and delicious fruit, but many of us spend much time looking for happiness around the next corner. We do not bend to enjoy the happiness which is ours for the taking just at our feet.

In our desire to reach the "pot of gold", complete and lasting happiness, we all want to fill our lives. We ignore anything which doesn't seem worthy of such a large **ambition**[2], or which can't give us the whole thing all at once.

Happiness is all around us, but it often comes in small **grains**[3]. When we gather it grain by grain, we soon have a basketful.

What small pieces of happiness surround me right now?

1. butterfly [ˈbʌtəflai] *n.* 蝴蝶
2. ambition [æmˈbiʃən] *n.* 野心;雄心
3. grain [ɡrein] *n.* 谷物;谷类

幸福在哪里

佚名

如今，我们要是用心寻找，就能找到幸福。幸福在心里，需要的只是表扬和重视。幸福源自内心。若快乐的思绪填满我们的大脑，努力看到事物的欢愉之处，我们就能与幸福携手。

金钱、财产或自满不能带给我们幸福。好车、豪宅、工作或某人，也不能使我们幸福。幸福是我们的精神状态，承认这点，安宁的心绪也便随之而至。幸福今日带给我们幸福永远。今天更有价值。

恐惧让我们无法感受欢乐与喜悦。左顾右盼和忧虑未来的持续状态，是我们最可怕的部分。试想一下，新配了一副眼镜，你的视力会得到改善，你会看得更清晰。考虑一下按着类似的方法调整自己的思维吧。当无用又无益的想法悄悄潜入你的意识，就将精力聚焦在快乐之事上，用更好更适合的思想替代它们吧。

心灵小语

米兰·昆德拉所说："衡量生命中的轻重是最模棱两难的。生活本身很复杂，但也可以很简单。认真是我们推崇的生活态度，可是，认真不等于严肃。轻盈地走过每一天，同样是生活中的一个很简单的道理。"幸福就是简单，就在我们心里！

美丽英文
Beautiful English

Where Is Happiness

Anonymous

We can find happiness today if we only look. Happiness is in our hearts and asks only to be **celebrated**[1] and valued. It comes from within. If we fill our mind with pleasant thoughts and try to look on the bright side, we invite happiness.

No amount of money, possessions, or ego **gratification**[2] can bring us happiness. There is no such thing as the perfect car, house, job, or person to make us happy. Peace of mind comes with the recognition that happiness is the state of mind we choose. Being happy today enables us to be happy forever. Today is what counts.

Our fears try to prevent us from feeling joy and pleasure. The fearful part of us would like us to be in a constant state of watching over our shoulder and of doubting the future. Imagine going to be fitted for new glasses. Your sight will be improved. You will see things more clearly. Consider adjusting your mind in a similar way. As unproductive, unhelpful thoughts **creep**[3] into your consciousness, replace them with better-fitting thoughts that focus on joy and pleasure.

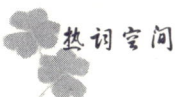
热词空间

1. celebrate ['selibreit] *v.* 庆祝;祝贺
2. gratification [ˌgrætifi'keiʃən] *n.* 满意
3. creep [kri:p] *v.* 爬;蹑手蹑脚;蔓延

当你觉得身心疲惫时,寻找一个心灵憩息之所,让自己得以片刻休息。

生活是一所全日制学校

A Full-time School Called Life

你是『生活』这所全日制学校的学生,每天都有机会学习各种课程。无论你喜欢与否,这些都是你的必修课。人各有志,每个人的人生目的和道路都不尽相同。在人生的旅途上,你需要不断地学习,只有这样,才有望实现人生目标。你所学的知识是特意为你而设的,而探寻人生意义、实现人生目标的关键则在于认真学习这些经验并汲取教训。

生命的启示

佚名

施与别人尽可能多的东西,并要欣然而为之。

牢记你最爱的诗歌。

不要相信你所听来的一切;也不要耗尽你所拥有的一切;更不要将时间都浪费在睡眠上。

说"我爱你"时,要满怀诚意。

说"对不起"时,要注视对方的眼睛。

至少在订婚半年后再结婚。

要笃信一见钟情。

对别人的梦想不妄加嘲讽,没有梦想的人不会拥有很多。

全心投入地去爱,或许你会受到伤害,可是,这却是使生活完整的唯一途径。

意见相悖时,要公正地争论,切不可大吵大嚷。

不要以一个人的亲戚来评判此人。

说话语速宜慢,但反应要快。

当有人问及你不想回答的问题时,要笑问对方:"为何想知道答案?"

谨记:不朽的爱情和伟大的成就要冒巨大风险才可获得。

要多打电话问候父母。

听到某人打喷嚏时,要说:"上帝保佑你。"

失败时,要记着汲取教训。

铭记 3R 原则,即:尊重自己,尊重他人,对自己的行为负责。

不可因小事而伤害友谊。

一旦意识到自己犯了错误,就要及时采取措施予以补救。

接听电话要保持微笑,因为对方可以从你的声音感受得到你的热情。

与有共同语言的人结为夫妻,那样在你年老时,就会发觉有共同的话题比其他

任何事情都更为重要。

给自己留些独处的时间。

勇于改变,但切不可放弃你的价值观。

记住:有时沉默是最好的回答。

多读书,少看电视。

过一种优质而高尚的生活,那样,当你逐渐老去,回首往事时,才会再次体味到生命的意义。

相信上帝,但要锁好你的车。

爱的氛围对一个家是何等重要,努力营造一个温馨和睦的家吧。

与至爱的人意见相左时,要恰当处理当前事态。

不要总翻旧账,过去的就让它过去吧。

要透过现象看事情的本质。

经常祈祷,它会使你力量倍增。

不要打断别人对你的溢美之言。

管好自己的事儿。

不可相信睁眼接受你亲吻的人。

一年当中,去一次你从未去过的地方。

倘若你发了财,要在有生之年用这些钱去帮助别人。

这是财富最伟大的满足。

谨记:塞翁失马,焉知非福?

谨记:伟大的友情往往都是付出的多,而索取的少。

判断一个人成功与否,要将他的办事能力与实际结果予以比较;而不是将他与别人作比较。要想得到情爱和食粮,就要不吝舍弃。

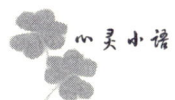

你的能力有多大,成功就有多大。要想得到更多的回报,就要不吝舍弃。所谓"鱼与熊掌,不可兼得",要想获得更大的胜利,就要适时放弃其他事情,要懂得分清主次,这样才可以做好更大的事情!

Instructions for Life

Anonymous

Give people more than they expect and do it cheerfully.

Memorize your favorite poem.

Don't believe all you hear, spend all you have or sleep all you want.

When you say, "I love you", mean it.

When you say, "I'm sorry", look the person in the eye.

Be engaged at least six months before you get married.

Believe in love at first sight.

Never laugh at anyone's dreams. People who don't have dreams don't have much.

Love deeply and passionately. You might get hurt but it's the only way to live life completely.

In disagreements, fight fairly. No name calling.

Don't judge people by their relatives.

Talk slowly but think quickly.

When someone asks you a question you don't want to answer, smile and ask, "Why do you want to know?"

Remember that great love and great achievements involve great risk.

Call your parents.

Say "bless you" when you hear someone sneeze.

When you lose, don't lose the lesson.

Remember the three R's: Respect for self; Respect for others; Responsibility for all your actions.

Don't let a little dispute injure a great friendship.

When you realize you've made a mistake, take immediate steps to correct it.

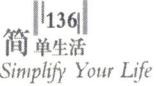

Smile when picking up the phone. The caller will hear it in your voice.

Marry a man/woman you love to talk to. As you get older, their conversational skills will be as important as any other.

Spend some time alone.

Open your arms to change, but don't let go of your values.

Remember that silence is sometimes the best answer.

Read more books and watch less TV.

Live a good, honorable life. Then when you get older and think back, you'll get to enjoy it a second time.

Trust in God but lock your car.

A loving atmosphere in your home is so important. Do all you can to create a tranquil harmonious home.

In disagreements with loved ones, deal with the current situation.

Don't bring up the past.

Read between the lines.

Pray. There's immeasurable power in it.

Never interrupt when you are being flattered.

Mind your own business.

Don't trust a man/woman who doesn't close his/her eyes when you kiss.

Once a year, go someplace you've never been before.

If you make a lot of money, put it to use helping others while you are living. That is wealth's greatest satisfaction.

Remember that not getting what you want is sometimes a stroke of luck.

Remember that the best relationship is one where your love for each other is greater than your need for each other.

Judge your success by what you have done compared to what you could have done, not to what others have done with their abilities.

Approach love and cooking with reckless abandon.

感悟生活

佚名

我知道了有时一个人想要的只是一只可握的手和一颗感知的心。

我知道了上帝并非一天完成所有的事,我又怎么可能呢?

我知道了治愈一切创伤的并非是时间,而是爱。

我知道了每一个与你相遇的人都值得你笑脸相迎。

我知道了和孩子睡在一起并用脸颊感觉他们的呼吸是最甜蜜的事。

我知道了只有当深爱一个人时才会认为他(她)是完美的。

我知道了机会从来不会自行消逝;别人会抓住你错过的机会。

我知道了当你内心痛苦时,幸福就可能停靠到别的港湾去。

我知道了我本应在母亲去世前再对她说一次我爱她。

我知道了一个人应谨慎地许下诺言,因为第二天他可能不得不食言。

我知道了微笑是改善容貌的一种并不昂贵的方式。

我知道了我无法选择我的感觉,但我可以选择做事方法。

我知道了每个人都想高踞山顶,但所有幸福和成长皆发生于爬山的过程中。

我知道了最好只在两种情况下给人以忠告:别人要求时和性命攸关时。

我知道了必须提高工作效率,我才可以做更多的事情。

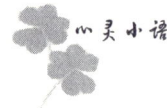

大多数人的生活由他们所处的环境决定。在这种环境中,我们寻找到许多能令自己开心的方法,并懂得珍视它们,让它们为自己服务。只要我们在既定的轨道上前进,把生活掌握在自己的手中,就会走好我们人生的每一步,并享受其中的幸福。

Word of Wisdom

Anonymous

I've learned that sometimes all a person needs is a hand to hold and a heart to understand.

I've learned that the Lord didn't do it all in one day. What makes me think I can?

I've learned that love, not time, heals all wounds.

I've learned that everyone you meet deserves to be greeted with a smile.

I've learned that there's nothing sweeter than sleeping with your babies and feeling their breath on your cheeks.

I've learned that no one is perfect until you fall in love with them.

I've learned that opportunities are never lost; someone will take the ones you miss.

I've learned that when you harbor bitterness, happiness will dock elsewhere.

I've learned that I wish I could have told my Mom that I love her one more time before she passed away.

I've learned that one should keep his words both soft and tender, because tomorrow he may have to eat them.

I've learned that a smile is an inexpensive way to improve your looks.

I've learned that I can't choose how I feel, but I can choose what I do about it.

I've learned that everyone wants to stand on top of the mountain, but all the happiness and growth occurs while you're climbing it.

I've learned that it is best to give advice in only two circumstances: when it is requested and when it is a life-threatening situation.

I've learned that the less time I have to work with, the more things I get done.

生命

拉尔夫·沃尔多·爱默生

生命可以被想象,但是不能被割裂,也不能被复制。生命的整体一旦被破坏就会引起混乱。灵魂不是孪生儿,而是独生苗。虽然它早晚都要像婴儿那样被孕育成熟,长得也像婴儿,却有着一种无敌的力量能决定命运,不会接受同一个生命。生命有着一种唯我独尊的神圣,这种神圣无须掩盖,每一天都显露在人们的举手投足之中。我们对自己深信不疑,但却怀疑别人。我们可以让自己为所欲为,但同样的事,别人做,我们称之为罪孽;我们只要自己来实验。我们充满自信的一个例子就是:人们从来不像他们想象的那样蔑视罪恶。换句话说,人人都为自己想好一个不受约束的自由,而这个自由是不能让别人来享用的。

行为从内在和外表,从性质和后果去看,各为不同。凶手行凶时所抱的意图决不像诗人以及传奇作家所描述的那样伤天害理,通常人们也觉察不出他心神不宁或诚惶诚恐的蛛丝马迹。行凶一事并不难谋划,但去考虑后果的话,它却能愈演愈烈,发出一系列丁当作响的恐怖声,把一切的关联都破坏。尤其是爱情所激发的罪行,从施罪者的角度看,似乎一切都理所当然,但这罪毕竟贻害社会。然而,还是没有人会最终相信犯罪的人是迷失了自我,还是没有人会认为那罪行如同重罪犯的所为那么恶不可赦。这是因为,就我们自身的情形而言,智力修正着道义判断,在智力的眼中,世上万事并无罪过。智力是反律法主义或超律法主义的,它判断着法律就像判断着事实一样。

生命是一样既抽象又具体的东西,让人既畏惧又渴望。生命不能被割裂,也不能被复制。人人都为自己想好一个不受约束的自由,而这个自由是不能让别人来与你共同享用的。

Life

Ralph Waldo Emerson

Life will be imaged, but cannot be divided nor doubled. Any invasion of its unity would be chaos. The soul is not twin-born, but the only begotten, and though revealing itself as child in time, child in appearance, is of a fatal and universal power, admitting no co-life. Every day, every act betrays the ill-concealed **deity**[1]. We believe in ourselves, as we do not believe in others. We permit all things to ourselves, and that which we call sin in others, is experiment for us. It is an instance of our faith in ourselves, that men never speak of crime as lightly as they think, or, every man thinks a latitude safe for himself, which is **nowise**[2] to be indulged to another.

The act looks very differently on the inside, and on the outside; in its quality, and its consequences. Murder in the murderer is no such ruinous thought as poets and romancers will have it; it does not unsettle him, or fright him from his ordinary notice of trifles: it is an act quite easy to be contemplated, but in its **sequel**[3], it turns out to be a horrible jangle and confounding all relations. Especially the crimes that spring from love, seem right and fair from the actor's point of view, but, when acted, are found destructive of society. No man at last believes that he can be lost, nor that the crime in him is as black as in the felon. Because the intellect qualifies in our own case the moral judgments. For there is no crime to the intellect. That is antinomian or hypernomian, and judges law as well as fact.

1. deity ['di:iti] *n.* 神;神性
2. nowise ['nəuwaiz] *adv.* 毫不;决不
3. sequel ['si:kwəl] *n.* 结局

人生絮语

佚名

在遇到心仪之人前,上帝也许会让我们先遇到其他不合适的人;这样,在我们最终遇见时,便会心存感恩。

当一扇幸福之门关闭时,另一扇便会开启。可多数时候,我们却因过久地凝望那扇紧闭的门,而忽略了为我们新敞开的那扇。

最好的朋友是那些与你心意相通的人,你会觉得你们的相对无言,是最美妙的心灵交流。

只有失去了,才知其珍贵;同样,只有拥有了,才发现其匮乏。这是至理名言。

施与真爱,不求回报,期待爱的传播,享受着对爱的自我满足。迷恋上一个人,需要一分钟;喜欢上她,需要一个小时;爱上她,需要一天;忘记她,则需要整整一生。

切勿追求外表的华美,它是不可靠的;切勿追求财富,它会灰飞湮灭。微笑,可以把光明洒向黑暗之隅,那么,追寻可以使你永远微笑的人,寻找能够使你会心而笑的人吧。

人的一生有许多这样的时刻:当你朝思暮想某人的时候,你恨不得把他从梦境中拉出来,与他真切地相拥于现实中!

生命不可轮回,机会不可再来,在有生之年,做自己想做的事,做自己想做的梦,去自己想去的地方,做自己想做的人吧。

愿快乐永远陪伴你,使你越发亲切可人;愿磨难时常伴随你,使你日渐坚强有力;愿心肺痛彻,令你人性通达;愿希望满怀,令你幸福快乐。

要经常换位思考，如果你感觉伤害到了自己，那么，可能别人也受到了伤害。

最幸福的人不一定拥有最美好的一切，他们只是最充分地珍惜了他们所拥有的一切。

幸福属于那些曾哭泣之人，曾受伤之人，不断探索之人。只有他们，才懂得对自己生活有影响的人们的重要性。

爱，起于微笑，浓于亲吻，逝于泪水。

光明的未来往往建立在对过去遗忘的基础之上。如果你总是沉湎于过去的失败和痛心中不能自拔，生活就不可能变得更加美好。

当你呱呱落地时，你哭着，周围的人都笑着。真诚地面对生活，那样，当你走到生命的尽头之时，才会是你笑着，周围的人哭着。

请把这些赠与对你的生命至关重要的那些人，那些曾影响你生活的人，那些给你微笑的人，那些在逆境中使你依然乐观向上的人，那些你想让他们知道你是多么珍惜与他们的情谊的人。即使你没有这样做，没关系，你不会因此倒霉，只是，用这些言语照亮他人生活的机会将与你失之交臂。

心灵小语

最好的朋友是那些与你心灵相通的人。生命不可轮回，机会不可再来，在有生之年，做自己想做的事，做自己想做的梦，去自己想去的地方，做自己想做的人，这才是真正的生活，才是我们真正需要的快乐！

Moving Thoughts

Anonymous

Maybe God wants us to meet a few wrong people before meeting the right one so that when we finally meet the right person, we will know how to be grateful for that gift.

When the door of happiness closes, another opens, but often times we look so long at the closed door that we don't see the one which has been opened for us.

The best kind of friend is the kind you can sit on a porch and **swing**[1] with, never say a word, and then walk away feeling like it was the best conversation you've every had.

It's true that we don't know what we've got until we lose it, but it's also true that we don't know what we've been missing until it arrives.

Giving someone all your love is never an **assurance**[2] that they'll love you back! Don't expect love in return; just wait for it to grow in their heart but if it doesn't, be content it grew in yours. It takes only a minute to get a crush on someone, an hour to like someone, and a day to love someone, but it takes a lifetime to forget someone.

Don't go for looks; they can deceive. Don't go for wealth; even that fades away. Go for someone who makes you smile because it takes only a smile to make a dark day seem bright. Find the one that makes your heart smile.

There are moments in life when you miss someone so much that you just want to pick them from your dreams and hug them for real!

Dream what you want to dream; go where you want to go; be what you want to be, because you have only one life and one chance to do all the things you want to do.

May you have enough happiness to make you sweet, enough trials to make you strong, enough **sorrow**[3] to keep you human, enough hope to make you happy.

Always put yourself in others' shoes. If you feel that it hurts you, it probably hurts the other person, too.

The happiest people don't necessarily have the best of everything; they just make the most of everything that comes along their way.

Happiness lies for those who cry, those who hurt, those who have searched, and those who have tried, for only they can **appreciate**[4] the importance of people who have touched their lives.

Love begins with a smile, grows with a kiss and ends with a tear.

The brightest future will always be based on a forgotten past, you can't go on well in life until you let go of your past failures and heartaches.

When you were born, you were crying and everyone around you was smiling. Live your life so that when you die, you're the one who is smiling and everyone around you is crying.

Please send this message to those people who mean something to you, to those who have touched your life in one way or another, to those who make you smile when you really need it, to those that make you see the brighter side of things when you are really down, to those who you want to let them know that you appreciate their friendship. And if you don't, don't worry, nothing bad will happen to you, you will just miss out on the opportunity to brighten someone's day with this message.

1. swing [swiŋ] v. 摇摆；摆动；旋转
2. assurance [ə'ʃuərəns] n. 确信；断言；保证
3. sorrow ['sɔrəu] n. 悲哀；悲痛
4. appreciate [ə'priːʃieit] v. 赏识；鉴赏；增值

平和的心态

佚名

月盈则亏,月晦则明。

第一次听到这句古语是中国寺庙中的一位僧侣告诉我的,它表达了一种平静的智慧,使我终生难忘。之后,每当压力和艰难降临到我身上时,或是遇到不可思议的成功或好运时,它都会让我以一颗平常心来对待,使我受益匪浅。这句古语带给我们的是一种希冀和安抚,即使痛苦和烦恼的阴霾再令人恐惧,也不会停留太久,同时也警示我们,不要过分在乎财富、权力和好运的光环,它们只会昙花一现。这种希冀和警示不仅适用于个人,同时也适用于政府、国家和领导人,它是人类的整个历史和经验的总结。此外,我们从中还可以听到使万物处于平衡中的法律和秩序的回声。

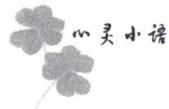
心灵小语

有些人寻找了一生,最终才知道平静的生活才是自己的追求;有些人为自己的人生勾画出一张宏伟的蓝图,虽然目标、理想明确,但是当他按着这个计划走下去时,却发现自己并不快乐。这是因为他缺少了一个重要因素——平和的心态。

A Good Measure of Equanimity

Anonymous

When the moon is fullest it begins to wane, when it is darkest it begins to grow. There is a calm wisdom in this old saying that impressed me when I heard it first from a **monk**[1] of a Buddhist **monastery**[2] in China. It has often, helped me to retain a good measure of **equanimity**[3] under stress and hardship as well as when some unexpected success or good luck might have made me too **exuberant**[4]. There is hope and consolation in the sure knowledge that even the darkest hours of pains and troubles won't last, but also a warning against **overrating**[5] the passing glories of wealth, power and great good fortune. A warning and a hope, not only for the individual, but also for governments, nations and their leaders, a brief **summing up**[6] of all that history and human experience can tell us. And beyond all that we might hear in it an echo of law and order that holds our universe in safe balance.

1. monk [mʌŋk] *n.* 修道士;僧侣
2. monastery [ˈmɔnəstri] *n.* 修道院;僧侣
3. equanimity [ˌiːkwəˈnimiti] *n.* 镇定
4. exuberant [igˈzjuːbərənt] *adj.* 繁茂的;丰富的;非凡的
5. overrate [ˈəuvəˈreit] *v.* 对估价过高
6. sum up *v.* 计算……的总数;概括;总结

我的生活真的那么糟吗

佚名

曾几何时,你是否有这样的感觉呢?生活是一团糟,真的太糟了,你渴望能有另一种环境。你发现生活对你来说很艰难,工作吃力,生活无味,一切都像是扭曲的。

读一读下面的故事吧,或许会改变你的人生观:

我和一个朋友结束谈话之后,他告诉我,尽管他做着两份工作,可每月的收入也只是刚过一千美圆,不过他还是快乐地生活。

他解释说这是因为在印度所看到的一件事……几年前,他经受了一次巨大的打击,情绪抑郁,就前往印度散心。

他说他亲眼目睹一位印度母亲用砍柴刀砍掉自己儿子的右手。母亲眼中的无助、四岁孩子的疼痛尖叫,直到今天还令他费解。

你或许会问,那位母亲为什么要这样做,是孩子淘气,还是孩子的右手被感染了?两者都不是,而仅仅是为了两个字——乞讨!绝望的母亲故意将孩子弄成残疾,这样孩子就可以上街乞讨。

我的朋友震惊了,他把吃了一半的面包掉在了地上。很快,五六个孩子一窝蜂地朝这片沾满沙粒的面包冲过来,争抢着——这是饥饿的自然反应。

朋友开始告诉自己,他是多么幸福。能有完整的身体、有工作、有家庭、有机会抱怨食物的好坏、有机会穿衣,可以拥有许多那些人欠缺的东西。

现在我也开始思索和感受,我的生活真得很糟吗?或许不是,我不应该觉得太糟。你觉得呢?或许下次你这样觉得时,就想想那位失去一只手的孩子,仅仅是因为能上街乞讨。"不要满足于你想得到的东西,而要满足于你已经拥有的东西。"

生活中有太多的无奈与不协调,这一切都源于不知足。珍惜,才是我们所要做的,不要再无视身边的一切,或许你还未发现它的重要,一旦失去,就会追悔莫及!

Is My Life Real Bad

Anonymous

Have you ever, at any one time, had the feeling that life is bad, real bad, and you wish you were in another situation? You find life make things difficult for you, work sucks, life sucks, everything seems to go wrong.

Read the following story, and it may change your views about life:

After a conversation with one of my friends, he told me despite taking 2 jobs, he brings back barely above 1,000 dollars per month, he is happy as he is.

He explained that it was through one incident that he saw in India... That happened a few years ago when he was really feeling low and touring India after a major setback.

He said that right in front of his very eyes, he saw an Indian mother chop off her child's right hand with a chopper. The helplessness in the mother's eyes, the scream of pain from the innocent 4-year-old child haunted him until today.

You may ask why did the mother do so; had the child been naughty, had the child's hand been infected? No, it was done for two simple words—TO BEG! The desperate mother deliberately caused the child to be handicapped so that the child could go out to the streets to beg.

Taken aback by the scene, he dropped a piece of bread he was eating half way. And almost instantly, a flock of 5 or 6 children swamped towards this small piece of bread which was covered with sand, robbing bits from one another—the natural reaction of hunger.

He began to tell himself how fortunate he is. How fortunate he is to be able to have a complete body, have a job, have a family, have the chance to complain what food is nice and what isn't nice. have the chance to be clothed, have the many things that these people in front of him are deprived of.

Now I begin to think and feel it, too! Was my life really that bad? Perhaps no, I should not feel bad at all. What about you? Maybe the next time you think you are, think about the child who lost one hand to beg on the streets. "Contentment is not the fulfillment of what you want, it is the realization of how much you already have."

生活给我上的一课

佚名

每当我遇到困难时,母亲就对我说:"如果你坚持下去,一切都会好的。不经历风雨,怎能见彩虹。"

直到1932年大学毕业,我才发现母亲是对的。当时我已决意在电台谋求发展,努力成为一名体育节目播音员。我搭便车抵达芝加哥后,开始奔波于各个电台之间——但被一一拒绝。

一位在播音室里工作的好心女士告诉我,大型的电台是不会冒险接纳毫无经验的新人——"到乡下去,找家能给你机会的小电台吧,"她说。

我乘车返回了家乡伊利诺斯州的迪克森。当时,家乡还没有电台播音员,父亲告诉我,蒙哥马利·沃德新开了家商店,正需要个管理体育部的当地运动员。上中学时,我曾在迪克森打过橄榄球,于是我申请了这份工作。我似乎挺适合做这项工作的,但结果却被拒绝了。

我失望极了。"一切总会好的,"母亲提醒我。为了方便找工作,父亲送我一辆汽车。我去爱荷华州的达文波特,到当地电台求职。那里的电台节目总监,苏格兰人彼得·麦克阿瑟告诉我,播音员已有合适的人选。

走出他的办公室时,挫折感油然而生。我大声说道:"如果在电台都找不到工作,又怎么能当体育节目的播音员呢?"

等电梯时,麦克阿瑟的声音传入我的耳畔,"你说什么体育呢!你懂橄榄球吗?"然后他让我到麦克风前,想象一场比赛,来做解说。

去年秋天，我们的球队赢得了一场比赛——在最后 20 秒的时间里以 65 码的距离获胜，我用 15 分钟将那场精彩的比赛解说下来。彼得对我说，我可以解说周六的那场比赛。

回家途中，母亲的话又在耳边响起，"坚持下去，终究会有转机。不经历风雨，怎能见彩虹？"我常想，当年，如果我能到蒙哥马利·沃德工作，我的人生又会驶向何方？

不经历风雨，怎能见彩虹。所谓阳光总在风雨后。付出了努力，才会有获得成功的机会。人生没有"天上掉馅饼"的事情，一切都要靠自己去创造！付出终有回报！

A Lesson of Life

Anonymous

"Everything happens for the best," my mother said whenever I faced disappointment. "If you can carry on, one day something good will happen. And you'll realize that it wouldn't have happened if not for that previous disappointment."

Mother was right, as I discovered after graduating from college in 1932, I had decided to try for a job in radio, then work my way up to sports announcer. I hitchhiked to Chicago and knocked on the door of every station—and got turned down every time.

In one studio, a kind lady told me that big stations couldn't risk hiring inexperienced person—"Go out in the sticks and find a small station that'll give you a chance," she said.

I **thumbed**[1] home to Dixon, Illinois. While them was no radio-announcing jobs in Dixon, my father said Montgomery Ward had opened a store and wanted a local athlete to manage its sports department. Since Dixon was where I had played high school football, I applied. The job sounded just right for me. But I wasn't hired.

My disappointment must have shown. "Everything happens for the best," Mom reminded me. Dad offered me the car to job hunt. I tried WOC Radio in Davenport, Iowa. The program director, a wonderful Scotsman named Peter MacArthur, told me they had already hired an announcer.

As I left his office, my **frustration**[2] boiled over. I asked aloud, "How can a fellow get to be a sport announcer if he can't get a job in a radio station?"

I was waiting for the elevator when I heard MacArthur calling, "What was that you said about sports? Do you know anything about football?" Then he stood me before a microphone and asked me to broadcast an imaginary game.

The **preceding**[3] autumn, my team had won a game in the last 20 seconds with a 65-yard run. I did a 15-minute **buildup**[4] to that play, and Peter told me I would be broadcasting Saturday's game!

On my way home, as I have many times since, I thought of my mother's words, "if you **carry on**[5], one day something good will happen. Something wouldn't have happened if not for that previous disappointment." I often wonder what direction my life might have taken if I'd gotten the job at Montgomery Ward.

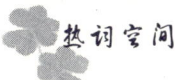

1. thumb [θʌm] v. 做搭车手势
2. frustration [frʌs'treiʃən] n. 挫败；挫折
3. preceding [pri'siːdiŋ] adj. 在先的；前面的
4. buidup ['bildʌp] n. 组合；集结；造舆论
5. carry on v. 继续开展；坚持；举止失常

体验生活

佚名

我懂得什么是欲望、奋斗、忧虑和绝望。我总是超负荷地工作。回望我的往昔生活,就如同战场般,到处充满了梦想与希望的断壁残垣。这场不利于我的战争使我伤痕累累,甚至早衰。

但我并不因此而怜悯自己;我没为过去伤心流泪;对于那些从未经历过我这样痛苦的女人,我也毫无嫉妒之感。因为我才是真正生活过,而她们仅仅是生存过。

我将生命之水一饮而尽,包括那些沉淀物,而她们只是浅尝了杯口的泡沫而已。她们不了解我所知道的,也不曾看到我所目睹的。

女人的眼睛只有被泪水冲刷过,才有更广阔的视野,才能在世界范围内有形同姐妹的朋友。

在充满艰辛曲折的社会大学中,我悟到了一条养尊处优的女人们所无从学到的哲理。我学会了"活在今天,而不无聊地透支明天的烦恼"。正是那种对未来的担忧使我们胆怯。因为经验告诉我,每当我非常害怕时,上天就会赋予我力量和智慧,于是,我不再胆怯。那些小小的烦恼再也无法影响我的行为——当你亲眼目睹了整座幸福大厦在你面前轰然坍塌后,那些诸如仆人忘了在洗手盆下放垫子,厨师不慎把菜汤弄洒之类的琐事,你就不会在意了。

我学会了不对人们寄予过高的期望,因而,我仍能从那些并不真诚的朋友和爱搬弄是非的人那里获取快乐。另外,我还具有了幽默感,因为此前的许多事情都使我大喜大悲。如果一个女人在困难面前不再歇斯底里,仍能保持幽默,那就不再有什么能伤害她了。

我丝毫不为经历过的困难而后悔,正因经历了这些,我才真正品味到多彩的生活。我为此所付出的一切是值得的。

生活是我们需要用心来体会的。真正珍惜过去的人,是不会悲叹旧日美好时光的逝去。因为藏于记忆中的时光永不流失。所以,在我们的有生之年,一定要向前看,要懂得享受生活带给我们的一切!

Experience Life

Anonymous

I have known want and struggle and anxiety and despair. I have always had to work beyond the limits of my strength. As I look back upon my life, I see it as a battle-field strewn with the wrecks of dead dreams and broken hopes and shattered illusions—a battle in which I always fought with the odds tremendously against me, and which has left me scarred and bruised and **maimed**[1] and old before my time.

Yet, I have no pity for myself; no tears to shed over the past and gone sorrows; no envy for the women who have been spared all I have gone through. For I have lived. They only existed.

I have drunk the cup of life down to its very dregs. They have only sipped the bubbles on top of it. I know things they will never know. I see things to which they are blind.

It is only the women whose eyes have been washed clear with tears who get the broad vision that makes them little sisters to all the world.

 I have learned in the great University of Hard Knocks a philosophy that no woman who has had an easy life ever acquires. I have learned to live each day as it comes and not to borrow trouble by dreading the morrow. It is the dark **menace**[2] of the future that makes cowards of us. I put that dread from me because experience has taught me that when the time comes that I so fear, the strength and wisdom to meet it will be given me. Little annoyances no longer have the power to affect me. After you have seen your whole edifice of happiness topple and crash in ruins about you, it never matters to you again that a servant forgets to put the **doilies**[3] under the finger bowls, or the cook spills the soup.

I have learned not to expect too much of people, and so I can still get happiness out of the friend who isn't quite true to me or the **acquaintance**[4] who **gossips**[5]. Above all, I have acquired a sense of humor, because there were so many things over which I had either to cry or laugh. And when a woman can joke over her troubles instead of having **hysterics**[6], nothing can ever hurt her much again.

I do not regret the **hardships**[7] I have known, because through them I have touched life at every point I have lived. And it was worth the price I had to pay.

1. maim [meim] v. 使残废；使不能工作
2. menace ['menəs] n. 威胁；危险物
3. doily ['dɔili] n. 小型装饰桌巾
4. acquaintance [ə'kweintəns] n. 相识；熟人
5. gossip ['gɔsip] n. 闲话；闲谈
6. hysteric [his'terik] n. 歇斯底里症之发作
7. hardship ['hɑːdˌʃip] n. 困苦；艰难；辛苦

草草行事的重要性

佚名

I. A. 威廉姆斯生于英格兰,在剑桥受过教育。第一次世界大战后,他成为伦敦泰晤士报的一名记者。威廉姆斯写了几本关于18世纪诗歌和戏剧方面的书,发表在各种期刊和杂志上,出版了他自己的诗集。以下这篇文章最早出现在1923年伦敦的《展望》一书中。

或许,对工作和创作而言,最大的威胁莫过于唯恐做得不好或者害怕做错。对于这个问题,这篇文章就是一种安慰了。威廉姆斯认为,很多事情都应该草草行事,这样,我们的生活才有意义,我们的个性才得以发展完善。运动和音乐就是两个很好的例子,大多数人都酷爱运动和音乐,它们的确能给人带来乐趣,仅是这一点就够了,人们并不需要有多深的造诣。

查尔斯·拉姆写了一系列有关时下谬误的文章。可惜我一时记不清了。但如果不是狡猾的仆人突然误导我,我倒不觉得他写过什么公众交口称赞而我却认为有害的文章。下面这句似是而非的忠告,我从孩提时就印在脑海中:"如果一件事情值得去做,那么,就应该好好去做。"

从没有哪一个谬论让人们如此热衷。因为世界上有很多事情都值得去做,但并不是事事都应该好好去做。伟大的哲人赫伯特·斯宾塞曾对刚在台球桌上战胜他的年轻人说:"先生,一般球技表现为好的眼力和稳定的手法,但从你的球技上看,你浪费了很多时间。"是否每一种游戏都值得持之以恒地练习和应用呢?

对职业运动员,我无话可说。他们是公众表演者,和其他人一样,他们通过自己在某项特定运动中的技术,至少可以实现人的首要社会责任——通过自己的合法劳动维持自己及家人的生活。但对于高明的业余爱好者,我们该怎么说呢?我认为,这些人是最应受到鄙视的。他们没有赚钱,仅仅为了自私的娱乐,就日复一日地投身于这种游戏。他们忽视了业余爱好者和专业人士之间合理的区别。最终他们为自己的技术所累,他们没做出任何对社会有价值的东西,没有垒起一片砖,没有犁过一亩地,没有写过一行文字,甚至没有通过劳动来养活全家和让自己受到教育。

不可否认,他们为某些人提供了娱乐,但他们一直没有勇气去参加测试。在这种测试中,我们需要每一个表演者证明他的职业选择是正确的——证明公众愿意为他的表演付费。当他们的辉煌期过去以后,不要说给整个世界留下什么,他们又给自己留下了什么呢?什么也没有留下,除了很快就会被遗忘的名字。也许他们的名字会被俱乐部里矮胖的绅士记住。

的确,玩游戏是一种并不值得好好去做的事情。

但这并不是说全然不值得去做,就像前面的谚语暗示我们的一样。没有什么比玩自己喜欢的游戏更惬意和更有益的了,哪怕玩不好也不会影响真正喜欢它的人的心情。太在乎输赢的人并不是真正的运动爱好者——这个观点很对,但它的含义并没被发掘。很少有人仅仅为了娱乐而玩游戏。为比赛而设的障碍为人们普遍接受,这不正好证明了这一点吗?为什么我们总是希望在自己的竞技能力之外额外得分呢?

"哦,但是,"我的读者也许会说,"弱一些的参赛者希望额外得分是为了促使强者有更好的表现。"但我并不这样认为。也许有时候,一个强壮但虚荣的参赛者希望给弱者额外加分,以使他的胜利更为显著。但我并不认为这是一个极好的解释。前些天去参加网球锦标赛时,我就把想法说给大赛秘书听了。"为什么要设置这些无聊的障碍呢?为什么不让我们尽情发挥?"我问他。"因为,"他回答道,"如果不设置这些障碍,就没有好一点的玩家参赛了。"这不就是承认了我们大多数人没有意识到草草行事的真正价值,还要固执己见、自欺欺人吗?

然而,并不是只有像游戏这样的小事才可以草草了之。虽然很奇怪,但事实是,我们易于接受草草地做某些事情,却不能接受草草地去做另一些事情。在我们认为可以草草去做的事情中,我举演戏为例,尽管演戏同其他表演艺术一样,会因其短暂性而减弱,但如果达到顶峰,也可以认为是一门伟大的艺术,一种值得好好去做的事情。演戏可以影响人类多变的情感,这就是演员所创造的东西——我们所说的表演艺术家是指能影响人类情感的有创造性的艺术家——是观众内心深处的一种印象、情感和思想，这是无法记录的。

所以，我认为，演戏可称得上是一种艺术，虽然我只是简单地拿出了我的论据。然而，是否有人因为演得不好而不允许进入业余的戏剧表演呢？从来没有！因为演戏就像我写这篇短文一样，是一种可以草草去做的事情。

另一种就是音乐。那句谚语的谬误在音乐上得到了验证。然而，不知为何，它在演戏上并没有得到验证。很多人认为如果他们不能唱出很动听的歌，不能很娴熟地弹奏钢琴或者小提琴、竖琴，那么，他们最好不要去做这些事情。我承认，他们不应该不加选择地把低劣的表演给公众或者他们的熟人看。但如果在家里也不能容忍这种低劣的音乐表演，这是我不赞成的。

没什么天赋的儿女，通过简单的歌声给她们的父母或不存在偏见的朋友带来快乐——这样的例子还少吗？然而有一天，这些小歌唱家开始因为不满足而苦恼。他们开始去学习音乐——如果他们资质平庸，性情温和——他们的局限就会暴露出来。十有八九，歌声就像一枚不值钱的硬币被抛在一边。有多少父亲为了鼓励女儿学歌而紧抓音乐不放？然而在教区音乐会上，她们可能会遭到打击。

在这里，我应该驻足观察一些奇怪的现象，有些人在画室或自家浴室从不唱歌，但在宗教集会或教堂里，他们会毫不犹豫地用那五音不全的嗓子放声高歌。我相信，要想回答这个问题，就得有一个完好的解释，但这属于神学的范畴，已经超出了我的研究范围。

"如果一件事值得去做，就应该好好去做"，这该死的说法就是导致个人生活极其匮乏的原因，从某种意义上讲，它也是公众生活水平降低的原因。这条谚语对资质平庸的人有两方面影响：它让资质平庸之辈不屑练习，而令资质超凡者为此付出很多，同时也将自己的思想强加给他人；它使人们疏于写作和写日记，同时也导致了本该锁在作者抽屉里的文集和日记的发表。

它导致了布兰克先生不去写诗——出于自娱自乐或与朋友的消遣，他可以写得很好的。同时，它也致使德茜小姐为了她那些并不成功的模仿之作（模仿德拉梅尔先生、叶芝先生和布里奇斯博士）而去纠缠各个杂志社疲惫的编辑们。结果是，现在，我们整个国家的艺术生活存在着两方面的迫切需求：更多的业余爱好者从事艺术实践，以及更高水平、更专业的艺术。只有达到这两个目标，我们才能获取心灵深处最美好的东西。

我认为,对我们来说,除去公民的职责,除去我们作为儿子、丈夫、父亲或者女儿、妻子、母亲的责任外,只有一件事情值得我们好好去做,值得我们全力以赴。这件事可以是写作、制造蒸汽机,也可以是砌砖块。除此之外,很多事我们都可以草草地去做,仅用我们一部分的精力,目的是为了放松自己或者触动自己的心灵。只有意识到这一点,人们才会幸福,才会满意,我们的家园才会更加美好。

我认为,有些事情草草去做可能比认真去做要好一些。比如钓鱼,其结果就是鱼儿被宰杀,一想到这些,钓鱼的乐趣就会荡然无存。当然,如果你既能钓到鱼又不去宰杀它,那就另当别论了。

心灵小语

很多事我们都可以草草地去做,用我们一部分的精力,达到放松自己或者触动自己心灵的目的。只有意识到这一点,我们才会幸福,才会满意,我们的家园才会更加美好,更加令人愉悦!

The Importance of Doing Things Badly

Anonymous

I. A. Williams was born in England and educated at Cambridge. After World War I he served as a **correspondent**[1] for the London Times. Williams wrote several books on eighteenth-century poetry and drama, published widely in journals and magazines, and published collections of his own poetry. The following article first appeared in London's *The Outlook* in 1923.

Perhaps the greatest threat to productivity in both work and play is the fear of doing things badly or wrong. This article offers some comfort. Williams points out that there are many things worth doing badly, and that our lives are enriched and our personalities enhanced by these activities. Two central examples, sports and music, are valuable to most people in proportion to how **enthusiastically**[2] they do them, rather than how well.

Charles Lamb wrote a series of essays upon popular fallacies. I do not, at the moment, carry them very clearly in my memory; but, unless that **treacherous**[3] servant misleads me more even than she usually does, he did not write of one piece of proverbial so-called wisdom that has always seemed to me to be peculiarly pernicious. And this saw, this scrap of specious advice, this untruth masquerading as logic, is one that I remember to have had hurled at my head at frequent intervals from my earliest youth right up to my present advanced age. How many times have I not been told that "If a thing is worth doing at all, it is worth doing well"?

Never was there a more untruthful word spoken in earnest. For the world is full of things that are worth doing, but certainly not worth doing well. Was it not so great a sage as

Herbert Spencer who said to the young man who had just beaten him at billiards, "Moderate skill, sir, is the sign of a good eye and a steady hand, but skill such as yours argues a youth misspent?" Is any game worth playing supremely well, at the price of constant practice and application?

Against the professional player I say nothing; he is a public entertainer, like any other, and by his skill in his particular sport he at least fulfills the first social duty of man—that of supporting himself and his family by his own **legitimate**[4] exertions. But what is to be said of the crack amateur? To me he seems one of the most contemptible of mankind. He earns no money, but devotes himself, for the mere selfish pleasure of the thing, to some game, which he plays day in day out; he breaks down the salutary distinction between the amateur and the professional; eventually his skill deserts him, and he leaves behind him nothing that is of service to his fellow men—not a brick laid, not an acre ploughed, not a line written, not even a family supported and educated by his labor.

It is true that he has provided entertainment for a certain number of persons, but he has never had the pluck to submit himself to the test by which we demand that every entertainer should justify his choice of a calling—the demonstration of the fact that the public is willing to pay him for his entertainment. And, when his day is over, what is left, not even to the world, but to himself? Nothing but a name that is at once forgotten, or is remembered by stout gentlemen in clubs.

The playing of games, certainly, is a thing which is not worth doing well.

But that does not prove that it is not worth doing at all, as the proverb would, by implication, persuade us. There is nothing more agreeable and salutary than playing a game which one likes, and the circumstance of doing it badly interferes with the pleasure of no real devotee of any pastime. The man who minds whether or not he wins is no true sportsman—which observation is trite, but the rule it implies is seldom observed, and comparatively few people really play games for the sheer enjoyment of the playing. Is this not proved by the prevalence and popularity of handicaps? Why should we expect to be given points unless it be that we wish to win by means other than our own skill?

"Ah! but," my reader may say, "the weaker player wants to receive points in order that he may give the stronger one a better game." Really, I do not believe that that is so. Possible, sometimes, a strong and **vainglorious**[5] player may wish to give points, in order that his victory may be the more notable. But I do not think that even this is the true explanation. That, I suspect, was given to me the other day by the secretary of a lawn-tennis tournament, in which I played. "Why all this nonsense of handicaps? Why not let us be squarely beaten, and done with it?" I asked him. "Because," He replied, "if we did not give handicaps, none of the less good players would enter." Is that not a confession that the majority of us have both realized the true value doing a trivial thing badly, for its own sake, and must needs have our minds buoyed and cheated into a false sense of excellence?

Moreover it is not only such intrinsically trivial things as games that are worth doing badly. This is a truth which, oddly enough, we accept freely of some things—but not of others—and as a thing which we are quite content to do will let me instance acting. Acting, at its best, can be a great art, a thing worth doing supremely well, though its worth, like that of all interpretative arts, is lessened by its **evanescence**[6]. For it works in the impermanent medium of human flesh and blood, and the thing that the actor create—for what we call an interpretative artist is really a creative artist working in a perishable medium—is an impression upon, an emotion or a thought aroused in, the minds of an audience, and is incapable of record.

Acting, then, let me postulate—though I have only sketched ever so briefly the proof of my belief—can be a great art. But is anyone ever deterred from taking part in amateur theatricals by the consideration that he cannot act well? Not a bit of it! And quite rightly not, for acting is one of the things about which I am writing this essay—the things that are worth doing badly.

Another such thing is music; but here the proverbial fallacy again exerts its power, as it does not, for some obscure and unreasoning discrimination, in acting. Most people seem to think that if they cannot sing, or play the piano, fiddle, or sackbut, admirably well, they must not do any of these things at all. That they should not indiscriminately force their inferior performances upon the public, or even upon their acquaintances, I admit. But that there is no place "in the home" for inferior musical performances, is an untruth that I flatly deny.

How many sons and daughters have not, with a very small talent, given their parents—and even the less fondly prejudiced ears of their friends—great pleasure with the singing of simple songs? Then one day there comes to the singer the serpent of dissatisfaction; singing lessons are taken, and—if the pupil is of moderate talent and modest disposition—limitations are discovered. And then, in nine cases out of ten, the singing is dropped, like a hot penny. How many fathers have not banished music from their homes by encouraging their daughters to take singing lessons? Yet a home may be the fresher for singing that would deserve brickbats at a parish concert.

I may pause here to notice the curious exception that people who cannot on any account be persuaded to sing in the drawing-room, or even in the bath, will without hesitation uplift their tuneless voices at religious meetings or in church. There is a perfectly good and honorable explanation of this, I believe, but it belongs to the realm of **metaphysics**[7] and is beyond my present scope.

This cursed belief, that if a thing is worth doing at all, it is worth doing well, is the cause of a great impoverishment in our private life, and also, to some extent, of the lowering of standards in our public life. For this tenet of proverbial faith has two effects on small talents: it leads modest persons not to exercise them at all, and immodest persons to attempt to do so too much and to force themselves upon the public. It leads to the decay of letter-writing and of the keeping of diaries, and, as surely, it leads to the publication of memoirs and diaries that should remain locked in the writers' desks.

It leads Mr. Blank not to write verses at all—which he might very well do, for the sake of his own happiness, and for the amusement of his friends—and it leads Miss Dash to pester the overworked editors of various journals with her unsuccessful imitations of Mr. de la Mare, Mr. Yeats, and Dr. Bridges. The result is that our national artistic life now suffers from two great needs: A wider amateur practice of the arts, and a higher, more exclusive, professional standard. Until these are achieved we shall not get the best out of our souls.

The truth is, I conceive, that there is for most of us only one thing—beyond, of course, our duties of citizenship and our personal duties as sons, or husbands, or fathers, daughters, or wives, or mothers—that is worth doing well—that is to say, with all our energy. That one thing may be writing, or it may be making steam-engines, or laying bricks. But after that there are hundreds of things that are worth doing badly, with only part of our energy, for the sake of the relaxation they bring us, and for the contacts which they give us with our minds. And the sooner England realizes this, as once she did, the happier, the more contented, the more gracious, will our land be.

There are even, I maintain, things that are in themselves better done badly than well. Consider fishing, where one's whole pleasure is often spoiled by having to kill a fish. Now, if one could contrive always to try to catch a fish, and never to do so, one might—But that is another story.

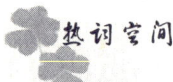

1. correspondent [ˌkɔrisˈpɔndənt] *n.* 通讯记者
2. enthusiastically [inˌθjuːziˈæstikəli] *adv.* 热心地
3. treacherous [ˈtretʃərəs] *adj.* 背叛的；叛逆的
4. legitimate [liˈdʒitimit] *adj.* 合法的；合理的
5. vainglorious [veinˈglɔːriəs] *adj.* 虚荣的
6. evanescence [ˌiːvəˈnesns] *n.* 逐渐消失
7. metaphysics [ˌmetəˈfiziks] *n.* 形而上学；玄学

做自己情绪的主人

佚名

潮涨潮落;冬去夏来;暑消寒长,日升日落;月圆月缺,雁来雁往;花开花谢,春种秋收。自然界万事万物都处于情绪的循环变化中,我是大自然的一部分,所以,我也有如潮水般的情绪,时涨时落。

很少有人懂得,这是大自然的一种愚弄。每天早晨,我醒来时,心情都与昨天有所不同。昨天的欢乐可能成了今天的悲伤,然而,今天的悲伤可能发展成明天的欢乐。在我的内心深处,好像有一个轮子,不断地从悲伤转到欢乐,从狂喜转到绝望,从快乐变为忧郁。就像花儿,今天绽放的喜悦会慢慢消退,变成明天凋谢的绝望,但是我会记住,今天枯萎的花朵同样孕育着明天绽放的种子,正如今天的悲伤也播种了明天的欢乐。

要让每一天都卓有成效,我该怎样控制这些情绪呢?如果我心浮气躁,那么这一天将会在失败中度过。植物树木的繁盛依赖于天气,但我创造着自己的天气,可以随时掌控。

那么我要怎样控制自己的情绪,让每一个日子充满快乐和成效呢?我要学会这个千古秘诀:行为受控于情绪的人是弱者,强者只会用行为控制情绪。每天醒来时,我要这样对抗悲伤、自怜、失败的情绪,这样才不会被它们俘虏——

如果我觉得沮丧,就放声歌唱。

如果我感到悲伤,就露出微笑。

如果我身体不适,就加倍工作。

如果我陷入恐惧,就埋头苦干。

如果我自惭形秽,就换上新装。

如果我犹疑不决,就提高分贝。

如果我囊中羞涩,就想象财富将至。

如果我力不从心,就回忆以往的成功。

如果我自轻自贱,就铭记自己的目标。

从今以后,我懂得,只有能力较低的人才会一直处于最佳状态,而我并非低能者。总有些时候,有些力量企图将我毁灭,而我必须不断地与之对抗。其中失望与悲伤很容易识破,但是,还有其他一些力量往往带着微笑靠近我,并向我伸出友谊之手,可它们却能将我毁灭。我同样要与它们抗争,永远不放弃对它们的掌控——

如果我骄傲自负,就追寻失败的记忆。

如果我沉湎享乐,就想想挨饿的过去。

如果我安于现状,就想想竞争对手。

如果我居功自傲,就回想屈辱之时。

如果我自以为是,就试着让风儿止步。

如果我腰缠万贯,想想那些食不果腹的人。

如果我目空一切,就想起自己怯懦的时候。

如果我不可一世,就抬起头来仰望群星。

从此,我能识别和辨认人类所有情绪变化的奥秘,包括自己的在内。从今以后,无论我的个人情绪如何变化,我都会随时做出积极的行动来控制。一旦我控制了自己的情绪,就掌握了自己的命运,也将成为自己的主人,变得卓尔不群。

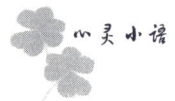
心灵小语

每个人都有自己的个性,有自己的情绪,他们都会跟随自己的性格做事,这样就会成就属于自己的成功。不应随波逐流,要擅于挖掘自己的独特性,从而创造新的灿烂!

美丽英文
Beautiful English

Today I Will be Master of My Emotions

Anonymous

The tides advance; the tides recede. Winter goes and summer comes. Summer wanes and the cold increases. The sun rises; the sun sets. The moon is full; the moon is black. The birds arrive; the birds depart. Flowers bloom; flowers fade. Seeds are sown; harvests are **reaped**[1]. All nature is a circle of moods and I am a part of nature and so, like the tides, my moods will rise; my moods will fall.

It is one of nature's tricks, little understood, that each day I awaken with moods that have changed from yesterday. Yesterday's joy will become today's sadness; yet today's sadness will grow into tomorrow's joy. Inside me is a wheel, constantly turning from sadness to joy, from exultation to depression, from happiness to **melancholy**[2]. Like the flowers, today's full bloom of joy will fade and withers into **despondency**[3], yet I will remember that as today's dead flower carries the seed of tomorrow's bloom so, too, does today's sadness carry the seed of tomorrow's joy.

And how will I master these emotions so that each day will be productive? For unless my mood is right the day will be a failure. Trees and plants depend on the weather to flourish but I make my own weather, yea I transport it with me.

And how will I master my emotions so that every day is a happy day, and a productive one? I will learn this secret of the ages: Weak is he who permits his thoughts to control his actions; strong is he who forces his actions to control his thoughts. Each day, when I awaken, I will follow this plan of battle before I am captured by the forces of sadness, self-pity and failure—

If I feel depressed I will sing.

If I feel sad I will laugh.

If I feel ill I will double my labor.

If I feel fear I will plunge ahead.

If I feel inferior I will wear new garments.

If I feel uncertain I will raise my voice.

If I feel poverty I will think of wealth to come.

If I feel incompetent I will remember past success.

If I feel insignificant I will remember my goals.

Henceforth, I will know that only those with inferior ability can always be at their best, and I am not inferior. There will be days when I must constantly struggle against forces which would tear me down. Those such as despair and sadness are simple to recognize but there are others which approach with a smile and the hand of friendship and they can also destroy me. Against them, too, I must never relinquish control—

If I become overconfident I will recall my failures.

If I overindulge I will think of past hungers.

If I feel complacency I will remember my competition.

If I enjoy moments of greatness I will remember moments of shame.

If I feel all-powerful I will try to stop the wind.

If I attain great wealth I will remember one unfed mouth.

If I become overly proud I will remember a moment of weakness.

If I feel my skill is unmatched I will look at the stars.

Henceforth I will recognize and identify the mystery of moods in all mankind, and in me. From this moment I am prepared to control whatever personality awakes in me each day. I will master my moods through positive action and when I master my moods I will control my destiny. I will become master of myself. I will become great.

热词空间

1. reap [riːp] *v.* 收割；收获
2. melancholy [ˈmelənkəli] *n.* 忧郁
3. despondency [diˈspɔndənsi] *n.* 失去勇气；失望

让内心的灯指引你

佚名

当你必须独自面对生活时，你一定要有足够的自信去追寻自己的梦想，并要做好准备为之有所牺牲。

你必须拥有改变自己和决定轻重缓急的能力，这样，你的最终目标才能实现。

有时，你需要挑战熟悉和安逸；有时，你需要抓住更多的机会，创造属于自己的未来。

你要足够坚强，至少，要试着使自己的生活更美好。

要相信自己不会轻易妥协、得过且过。

要欣赏自己，给自己成长、发展的机会，并找到自己生活的真正意义。

不要活在别人的阴影里，属于你的阳光会指引你前进的道路。

努力去做自己喜欢做的事，努力克服所有的障碍。

笑对自己的过失，从中汲取教训，并引以为豪。

摘些花朵，欣赏大自然的美。

向陌生人问好，享受熟人的陪伴。

别害怕流露真情，放声大笑、纵情哭泣，会让你感觉更好。

全心全意地爱你的家人、朋友，他们是你生活中最重要的部分。

在阳光灿烂的日子里，感受安宁。

寻找彩虹，活在梦想的世界，永远记住，生活比看上去的更美好。

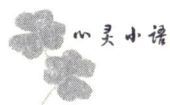

心灵小语

当你必须独自面对生活时，你一定要有足够的自信去追寻自己的梦想，并做好准备为之有所牺牲；你要足够坚强，要相信自己不会轻易妥协、得过且过。这样你的生活才会更美好。

Allow Your Own Inner Light to Guide You

Anonymous

There comes a time when you must stand alone. You must feel confident enough within yourself to follow your own dreams. You must be willing to make sacrifices.

You must be capable of changing and rearranging your priorities, so that your final goal can be achieved.

Sometimes, familiarity and comfort need to be challenged. There are times when you must take a few extra chances and create your own realities.

Be strong enough to at least try to make your life better.

Be confident enough that you won't settle for a compromise just to get by.

Appreciate yourself by allowing yourself the opportunities to grow, develop, and find your true sense of purpose in this life.

Don't stand in someone else's shadow when it's your sunlight that should lead the way.

Work hard at what you like to do and try to overcome all obstacles.

Laugh at your mistakes and praise yourself for learning from them.

Pick some flowers and appreciate the beauty of nature.

Say hello to strangers and enjoy the people you know.

Don't be afraid to show your emotions, laughing and crying make you feel better.

Love your friends and family with your entire being they are the most important part of your life.

Feel the calmness on a quiet sunny day.

Find a rainbow and live your world of dreams, always remember life is better than it seems.

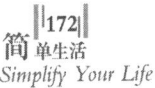

保持平静小贴士

佚名

老人慢慢地数着硬币,一个,两个……我盯着他颤抖的手指,恼怒地叹着气,不耐烦地在结账的队伍里晃着身子。听到了我的叹息声,他抱歉地笑了笑——那是一种羞愧的笑,是一种因自己的衰弱耽误了社会事务而内疚的笑容。

那刻,我后悔极了。我想,终有一天自己也会像他那样,需要陌生人的善意。于是,我拍了拍他磨损的衣袖,说:"别急,慢慢来。"

接着,我想起了自己很多次都缺乏耐性——绿灯一亮就按喇叭,尖刻地批评反应慢的人。缺乏耐性有什么大不了的吗?是的,这样不行。不耐烦时,你很容易表现得粗鲁,这种行为会引起他人恼火、固执或不合作等不良结果。

于是,我决定耐心点,也想出了在紧迫情形下能使自己平静的种种办法。我不敢说这些方法会让我脱胎换骨,耐性十足,但至少它们能帮我消除生活中的某些烦躁,并在大多数场合控制住情绪。

容许稍有差错

一个朋友通过了一份重要工作的面试。为了以防万一,还需让公司总裁与他的妻子见个面。

6点钟时,朋友和他的妻子进入通往纽约的隧道,赶赴7点钟与总裁的约会。7点了,他们还被困在隧道,前方的路被一辆翻倒的拖车堵住了。当他们赶到宾馆时,总裁已经走了,没有留下只字片言。第二天,他也不听任何解释,只是说:"你们应该考虑到路上可能会有事情耽搁。"

没耐性的人不愿浪费时间,所以他们把任何事都安排得过于紧凑。他们精确计算着每次旅行的行程和一次任务所花的时间,根本不考虑发生耽搁或意外情况的可能性。我们最好为差错留出余地。要赶赴的约会越重要,就越要把时间安排充裕。如果某个约会极为重要,那就很值得花时间了。

要换个角度来看问题

理想的工作没有争取到确实很遗憾,但很少有特别严重的事是因延误造成的。因此,我们也不必烦躁不安。

我懂得这样问自己:"最坏可能会发生什么?"如果最坏也只是错过电影开头的演员表演部分或是球赛的开场,我就会使自己平静下来。今天迟到了10分钟,下周我仍会记得吗?换个角度看问题就能消除急躁的情绪。

要提前规划好一切

一天傍晚,我的一个熟人准备周末外出旅行,但汽车发动不了——与此同时,她的三个朋友正在街角处等着她来接,但她没法联系上他们。当她一小时后赶到时,焦急万分的朋友们已经冻得瑟瑟发抖,可怜兮兮的。她的尴尬经历让我领悟了一些道理,在这之后,我总把约会安排在易于联系的地方,以防意外情况而延误。这样,我就能在事情出错时,还能保持耐性。

要提前做好准备

现代生活中,最折磨人的事情莫过于在机场候机。一天清晨,在罗利—达勒姆国际机场,我正看着雨水沿玻璃窗奔流而下。这时,一个人走了过来,他从口袋里掏出一份猜字游戏,问我想不想玩。在飞机晚点的4个钟头里,我们兴致勃勃地玩着猜字游戏。旁边的一位男士在用手提电脑工作。一位女士慢条斯理地浏览了一大叠目录,并把页脚折记上,填好订购单。最没耐性的人在候机区里踱来踱去,而那些无所事事、只会往自动售货机里投币的人则在那里大声地抱怨着。

而今,我总假定路上有耽搁情况,所以,我总会带上一本书,朋友则总带着填字游戏玩。

要享受当前时刻

我认识一个人,他总是急不可待地做下一步事情。工作之余,如果我们要一起喝喝酒,他首先会问我们到哪里吃饭;吃饭时,他仓促地吃下点心,就匆忙赶往电影院;电影最后一幕还未结束,他就起身离开了;开车回家路上,他就为第二天、下周乃至明年做计划了。

他从未活在当前时刻,也便享受不到生活的乐趣。

我已经领会到,生活有其自己的时刻表。孕育一个孩子需9个或10个月,把他抚养成人则需21年。要成为一名出色的小提琴手或滑雪运动员,需要相当长的时间。取得成功也需要时间,而要成为一名成功人士,则更是一个漫长的过程。

或许,控制急躁情绪的最后一招是确定这种情绪是否来源于自身。你是否不愿给孩子一些时间去学习呢?或者,对于行动迟缓的人,你根本不想给他完成工作的时间?如果你只是偶然没耐性,那么,你的烦恼就会即刻烟消云散;如果你总是易怒,可能是觉得自己最重要,自己的事情重于一切。

当然,你没有那么重要,谁也不会那么重要。假如我们能接受这一点——世界是供我们细细品味,而不是为我们提供方便的——我们就能过得更加平和,也会对生活中的点点滴滴更有耐心。于是,我们就会成为他人——也是自己的好伙伴。

如果你只是偶尔没耐性,你的烦恼就会即刻烟消云散;如果你总是易怒,可能是觉得自己最要,自己的事情重于一切。理想的工作没有争取到确实很遗憾,但很少有特别严重的事是因延误造成的。因此,我们不必烦躁不安。

Tips for Staying Calm

Anonymous

I watched the old man's fumbling fingers as he slowly counted out the coins, one by one. I was all but dancing with impatience in the checkout line and sighed with **exasperation**[1]. Hearing me, he smiled apologetically—a tiny smile of **humiliation**[2] at being feeble and holding up the world's business.

Then I became contrite. Putting myself in his shoes, I realized that someday they might pinch my feet. I too, could become dependent on the kindness of strangers. I patted his frayed sleeves "Take your time," I said, "there's no hurry."

It occurred to me how often I have acted impatiently—honking my horn the instant the light changed, speaking sharply to someone slow to understand. Did it matter? It did. When you're impatient, you're apt to be rude. And such behavior is counter-productive, making people angry or **stubborn**[3] or uncooperative.

I decided to try becoming more patient and to develop various approaches for calming myself in stressful situations. I can't claim that these techniques transformed me into a model of patience, but they have helped me eliminate some impatience from my life and control most of it.

Allow for a margin of error

A friend had passed the interviews for an important new job; all that remained was for the president of the company to meet his wife.

At six, my friend and his wife were in the tunnel on their way into New York for a seven o'clock appointment. At seven, they were still in the tunnel, stuck behind an overturned tractor-trailer. When they finally reached the president's hotel, he had gone, leaving no message. He would not accept an explanation the next day. "You should have planned for delays," he said.

Impatient people don't like to waste time, so they cut things too closely. They budge the exact number of minutes that a journey or task should take, not allowing for the possibility of delay or the unexpected. It is better to provide a margin for error. The more important your appointment is, the more time should be allotted. When an appointment absolutely can't be missed, it pays to allow ridiculous amounts of time.

Put things in perspective

Not setting a coveted job is calamitous, but the consequences of being held up are seldom that serious. They are not worth getting impatient.

I've learned to ask myself, "What's the worst that can happen?" If the answer is that I'll miss the opening credits of a movie or the start of a ball game, I calm down. Will I even remember next week that I was ten minutes late today? Putting matters in perspective should ease your impatience.

Think ahead

One evening as an acquaintance was leaving for a weekend trip, her car wouldn't start—and three friends were waiting to be picked up on a street corner. She had no way of getting word to them; they were cold and miserable and worried when she arrived an hour late. Since hearing her **predicament**[4], I've always arranged to meet people where they or I can be reached in case of delay. It enables me to be far more patient when things go wrong.

Be prepared

Waiting in airports is one of the most trying features of modern life. I was watching torrential rains streak the windows at Raleigh-Durham International Airport one morning when a man came up, took a word game from his pocket and asked if I wanted to play. We played with pleasure for the four hours our plane was delayed. Near us, a man worked on his laptop computer. One woman went through a stack of catalogues methodically, turning down the corners of the pages, filling out order blanks. The most impatient people—the ones who prowled the waiting area and complained loudly—were those who had nothing to do but put coins in the vending machines.

I now assume I'll encounter a delay, so I always carry a paperback. A friend works crossword puzzles.

Live for the moment

A man I knew was always racing impatiently into the future. If we met for a drink after work, the first thing he talked about was where we'd go for dinner; at dinner, he rushed through **dessert**[5] to get to a movie; at the movie, he was on his feet before the last frame faded. And in the car on the way home, he was making plans for the next day, next week, next year.

Never did he live in the here and now. Consequently, he couldn't enjoy life.

I've come to appreciate that life has its own timetable. It takes nine or ten months to make a baby, 21 years to make an adult. It takes a long time to become a good violinist or downhill skier. It also takes time to become a success and even more time to become a success as a person.

Perhaps the last thing for controlling impatience is to examine your own contribution to it. Are you unwilling to grant children time to learn, or slow people time to accomplish a task? If impatience is only occasional, your annoyance will pass. But if you're almost always irritable and abrupt, you may well feel that you're just too important to ever be kept waiting for anyone or anything.

You're not, of course; none of us are. If we can accept that the world is ours to enjoy but not made for our convenience, we'll be better able to move through it equably, more patient with the ordinary vicissitudes of life and a good companion to our fellow human beings and to ourselves.

热词空间

1. exasperation [igˌzɑːspəˈreiʃən] *n.* 恼怒
2. humiliation [hjuːˌmiliˈeiʃən] *n.* 羞辱；蒙耻
3. stubborn [ˈstʌbən] *adj.* 顽固；固执；坚定
4. predicament [priˈdikəmənt] *adj.* 困境
5. dessert [diˈzəːt] *n.* 餐后甜点

论宁静的心境

约叔亚·罗斯·李普曼

曾经,当我是一个充满了丰富幻想的年经人时,着手起草了一份被公认为人生"幸福"的目录。就像别人有时会将他们所拥有或想要拥有的财产列成表一样,我将世人希求之物列成表:健康、爱情、美丽、才智、权力、财富和名誉。

当我完成清单后,我自豪地将它交给一位睿智的长者,他曾是我少年时代的良师和精神楷模。或许我是想以此来加深他对我早熟智慧的印象。无论如何,我把单子递给了他。我充满自信地对他说:"这是人类幸福的总和。一个人若能拥有这些,就和神差不多了。"

在我朋友老迈的眼角处,我看到了感兴趣的皱纹,汇聚成一张耐心的网。他深思熟虑后说:"是一张出色的表单,内容整理详细,记录顺序也合理。但是,我的年轻朋友,好像你忽略了最重要的一个要素。你忘了那个要素,如果缺少了它,每项财产都会变成可怕的折磨。"

我立即暴躁地逼问:"那么,我遗漏的这个要素是什么?"

他用一小段铅笔划掉我的整张表格。在一拳击碎我的少年美梦之后,他写下三个单词:心之静,"这是上帝为他特别的子民保留的礼物。"他说道。

"他赐予许多人才能和美丽。财富是平凡的,名望也不稀有,但心灵的宁静才是他允诺的最终赏赐,是他爱的最佳象征。他施予它的时候很谨慎。多数人从未享受过,有些人则等待了一生——是的,一直到高龄,才等到赏赐降临他们身上。"

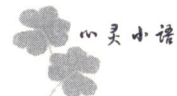

生活是我们忙于制定其他计划时所发生的一切。我们因忙碌而失去许多本该幸福的东西,当我们与他人争论不休时,既浪费时间,又毫无益处,会对身心健康造成很大的伤害,所以最重要的是我们要把握住本该珍惜的东西,这才是衡量我们内心世界是否宁静的一个标准。

On Peace of Mind

Joshua Loth Liebman

Once, as a young man full of exuberant fancy, I undertook to draw up a catalogue of the acknowledged "goods" of life. As other men sometimes tabulate lists of properties they own or would like to own, I set down my inventory of earthly desirables: health, love, beauty, talent, power, riches, and fame.

When my inventory was completed I proudly showed it to a wise elder who had been the mentor and spiritual model of my youth. Perhaps I was trying to impress him with my precocious wisdom. Anyway, I handed him the list. "This", I told him confidently, "is the sum of mortal goods. Could a man possess them all, he would be as a god."

At the corners of my friend's old eyes, I saw wrinkles of amusement gathering in a patient net. "An excellent list," he said, pondering it thoughtfully. "Well digested in contented and set down in not–unreasonable order. But it appears, my young friend, that you have omitted the most important element of all. You have forgotten the one ingredient, lacking which each possession becomes a hideous torment."

"And what," I asked, peppering my voice with truculence, "is that missing ingredient?"

With a pencil stub he crossed out my entire schedule. Then, having demolished my adolescent dream structure at a single stroke, he wrote down three syllables: peace of mind. "This is the gift that God reserves for His special proteges," he said.

"Talent and beauty He gives to many. Wealth is commonplace, fame not rare. But peace of mind—that is His final guerdon of approval, the fondest insignia of His love. He bestows it charily. Most men are never blessed with it; others wait all their lives—yes, far into advanced age—for this gift to descend upon them."

生活是一所全日制学校

佚名

你是"生活"这所全日制学校的学生,每天都有机会学习各种课程。无论你喜欢与否,这些都是你的必修课。

为什么你会生活在这里?你生活的目的何在?长久以来,人们都在探寻人生的意义。然而,每一代人都忽略了一个事实——人生的意义并不是一个答案,它是因人而异的。

人各有志,每个人的人生目的和道路都不尽相同。在人生的旅途上,你需要不断地学习,只有这样,才有望实现人生目标。你所学的知识是特意为你而设的,而探寻人生意义、实现人生目标的关键则在于认真学习这些经验并汲取教训。

在生命旅程中,别人不必面对的挑战和教训,你或许要面对;当然,别人为之奋斗多年的诸多挑战,你也许不必应对。你拥有幸福的婚姻,而你的朋友却要饱尝婚姻之苦,承受离婚之痛,这些你大概永远都没法弄明白。同样,对于你疲于奔命,却过着拮据的生活,而你的朋友却过着安逸优越的生活,你也可能无法理解。但有一点是肯定的,就是那些注定要学的知识与经验你定会有缘相识。至于是否愿意学,则完全取决于你自己。

因此,这里的挑战在于你要汲取各种不同的经验和教训,以使你的生活符合自己独特的人生道路。这是你一生都要面对的最严峻的挑战。之所以这样说,是因为人生道路各有差别。但是,谨记——不要与周围的人相比,计较不同的经验和教训;你要学的东西是你力所能及的,并且是特意为你的成长量身定制的。

事事公正、人人平等是我们的愿望,这即是所谓的公平感。然而,事实上,生活并非总是公平的,或许命运不应该这样安排,但你的人生就是有可能比别人艰辛、坎坷。每个人的情况不同,所以,也该用不同的方法对待自己的境遇。若想拥有平和的心境,就不可存有悲观厌世的心态。过于计较世事的不公,容易自轻自贱,从而发现不了自己的独特之处。因受愤世嫉俗、懊恼烦闷的情绪干扰,你也许会错过许多自己该学的课程。

心灵小语

我们中的大多数人认为生活是理所当然的。我们知道总有一天我们要面对死亡,但总认为那一天还在遥远的将来。当我们身强体健之时,死亡似乎是不可想象的,我们很少考虑它。日子多的好像没有尽头。因此,我们一味忙于琐事,却没感觉到这样对待生活的态度太盲目。所以,我们每一个人都要汲取各种不同的经验和教训,使自己的生活符合自己独特的人生道路。

美丽英文
Beautiful English

A Full-time School Called Life

Anonymous

You are enrolled in a full-time school called "life". Each day in this school you will have the opportunity to learn lessons. You may like the lessons or hate them, but you have designed them as part of your **curriculum**[1].

Why are you here? What is your purpose? Humans have sought to discover the meaning of life for a very long time. What we and our ancestors have overlooked, however, is that there is no one answer. The meaning of life is different for every individual.

Each person has his or her own purpose and distinct path, unique and separate from anyone else's. As you travel your life path, you will be presented with **numerous**[2] lessons that you will need to learn in order to **fulfill**[3] that purpose. The lessons you are presented with are specific to you; learning these lessons is the key to discovering and fulfilling the meaning and relevance of your own life.

As you travel through your lifetime, you may **encounter**[4] challenging lessons that others don't have to face, while others spend years struggling with challenges that you don't need to deal with. You may never know why you are blessed with a wonderful marriage, while your friends suffer through bitter arguments and painful divorces, just as you cannot be sure why you struggle financially while your peers enjoy abundance. The only thing you can count on for certain is that you will be presented with all the lessons that you are capable of you specifically need to learn; whether you choose to learn them or not is entirely up to you.

The challenge here, therefore, is to align yourself with your own unique path by learning individual lessons. This is one of the most difficult challenges you will be faced with in your lifetime, as sometimes your path will be **radically**[5] different from others. But, remember, don't compare your path to the people around you and focus on the disparity between their lessons and yours. You need to remember that you will only be faced with lessons learning and are specific to your own growth.

Our sense of fairness is the expectation of equity—the assumption that all things are equal and that justice will always prevail. Life is not, in fact, fair, and you may indeed have a more difficult life path than others around you, deserved or not. Everyone's circumstances are unique, and everyone needs to handle his or her own circumstances differently. If you want to move toward **serenity**[6], you will be required to move out of the complaining phase of "it's not fair". Focusing on the unfairness of circumstances keeps you comparing yourself with others rather than appreciating your own special uniqueness. You miss out on learning your individual lessons by distracting yourself with feelings of bitterness and resentment.

1. curriculum [kəˈrikjuləm] *n.* 课程
2. numerous [ˈnjuːmərəs] *adj.* 众多的;许多的
3. fulfill [fulˈfil] *v.* 履行;实现;完成
4. encounter [inˈkauntə] *v.* 遭遇;遇到
5. radically [ˈrædikəli] *adv.* 根本上;以激进的方式
6. serenity [siˈreniti] *n.* 平静

一生的收获

佚名

他11岁那年，一有机会就到新汉普郡湖心岛上自家小屋的码头钓鱼。在鲈鱼季节到来的前一天，他和父亲晚上很早就开始准备了。他们用小虫做诱饵来钓太阳鱼和鲈鱼。他在银色的鱼钩上放好诱饵，开始练习抛线。鱼钩撞到水面上，在夕阳中荡起一片色彩斑斓的水波。接着，当月亮升起来时，水波就变得银光闪闪的。

当他的鱼杆弯下去的时候，他知道线的那一端一定钓到了一条大鱼。他灵巧地在码头边沿和那条大鱼周旋。父亲用充满赞赏的眼神看着他。

最后，他很小心地将那条筋疲力尽的鱼从水里拉了出来。这可是他所见过的最大的一条鱼，而且还是一条鲈鱼。

男孩和他的父亲凝视着这条漂亮的鱼，它的鳃在月光下一张一翕。父亲点亮一根火柴，看了一下表。现在是晚上10点——离鲈鱼季节的开放还有两个小时。他看了看鱼，又看了看那个男孩。

"你要把它再放回去，儿子。"他说。

"爸爸！"男孩喊。

"还会有其他鱼的。"父亲说。

"但肯定不会像这条一样大，"男孩喊道。

他看了看湖的周围。在月光的笼罩下，周围没有其他的渔民或船只。他再一次看着父亲。尽管并没有人看着他们，也没有人知道他们是什么时候钓到鱼的，但从父亲那坚定的声音中，男孩知道这个决定是不可更改的。他慢慢地将鱼钩从大鲈鱼的唇上拿下来，然后蹲下来把那条鱼放回水里。

那条鱼摆了摆它强健的身子，消失在水里。男孩怀疑他再也不可能看到那么大的鱼了。

那件事已经过去34年了。而今,那个男孩已经成为纽约城里一位成功的建筑师。他父亲的小屋仍然矗立于湖心岛上。他也曾带着自己的儿子和女儿回到同一个码头去钓鱼。

他当时的猜想是对的。他再也没有见过那么大的鱼了,大如很久以前的那天晚上所钓到的那条鱼。但是,在他每次面对道德问题时,那条大鱼总会浮现在他的眼前。

因为正如父亲告诉他的那样,道德是简单的对和错的问题,但困难的是付诸行动。在旁侧无人时,我们能否仍然正当行事?我们是否会拒绝为了按时完成设计而草率了事?或者在明知不应该的情况下,我们是否会根据不该得知的信息买卖公司股票?

当我们年轻的时候,如果有人要让我们把鱼放回去,我们就会那样去做,因为我们从中将学到真理。选择去做正确事情的决定将在我们的记忆里变得深刻而清晰。我们可以把这个故事自豪地讲给我们的朋友和后辈听。这不是关于如何攻击某种体制并战胜它,而是关于如何去做正确的事情,从而变得更加坚强有力。

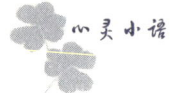 心灵小语

道德是简单的对和错的问题,但困难的是付诸行动。在旁侧无人时,我们能否仍然正当行事?我们是否会拒绝为了按时完成设计而草率了事?

Catch of a Lifetime

Anonymous

He was 11 years old and went fishing every chance he got from the dock at his family's cabin on an island in the middle of a New Hampshire lake.

On the day before the **bass**[1] season opened, he and his father were fishing early in the evening, catching sunfish and perch with worms. Then he tied on a small silver **lure**[2] and practiced casting. The lure struck the water and caused colored ripples in the sunset, then silver ripples as the moon rose over the lake.

When his peapole doubled over, he knew something huge was on the other end. His father watched with admiration as the boy skillfully worked the fish alongside the dock.

Finally, he very gingerly lifted the exhausted fish from the water. It was the largest one he had ever seen, but it was a bass.

The boy and his father looked at the handsome fish, gills playing back and forth in the moonlight. The father lit a match and looked at his watch. It was 10 P.M. —two hours before the season opened. He looked at the fish, then at the boy.

"You'll have to put it back, son." he said.

"Dad!" cried the boy.

"There will be other fish." said his father.

"Not as big as this one." cried the boy.

He looked around the lake. No other fishermen or boats were anywhere around in the moonlight. He looked again at his father. Even though no one had seen them, nor could anyone ever know what time he caught the fish, the boy could tell by the clarity of his father's voice that the decision was not **negotiable**[3]. He slowly worked the **hook**[4] out of the lip of the huge bass and lowered it into the black water.

The creature swished its powerful body and disappeared. The boy suspected that he would never again see such a great fish.

That was 34 years ago. Today, the boy is a successful architect in New York City. His father's cabin is still there on the island in the middle of the lake. He takes his own son and daughters fishing from the same dock.

And he was right. He has never again caught such a magnificent fish as the one he landed that night long ago. But he does see that same fish again and again —every time he comes up against a question of ethics.

For, as his father taught him, ethics are simple matters of right and wrong. It is only the practice of ethics that is difficult. Do we do right when no one is looking? Do we refuse to cut corners to get the design in on time? Or refuse to trade stocks based on information that we know we aren't supposed to have?

We would if we were taught to put the fish back when we were young. For we would have learned the truth. The decision to do right lives fresh and **fragrant**[5] in our memory. It is a story we will proudly tell our friends and grandchildren. Not about how we had a chance to beat the system and took it, but about how we did the right thing and were forever strengthened.

热词空间

1. bass [beis] *n.* 一种欧洲产的鲈鱼
2. lure [ljuə] *v.* 引诱
3. negotiable [ni'gəuʃjəbl] *adj.* 可协商的；可通行的
4. hook [huk] *n.* 钩；吊钩
5. fragrant ['freigrənt] *adj.* 芬芳的；香的

生 活

佚名

生活不是积分。你有多少朋友或你受大家欢迎的程度与它无关。

这个周末你是有安排还是独自度过也与它无关。

你现在正与谁约会,你曾经与谁约会,你曾与多少人约会,或者你从未与谁约会,都与它无关。

你曾吻过谁,与它无关。

它也无关两性问题。

不是关于谁是你的家人,或者他们有多少钱。

或者你开哪种车。

或者你在哪上学。

你有多漂亮或多丑陋与它无关。

或者,你穿什么样的衣服,有什么样的鞋子,听哪种类型的音乐,都跟它无关。

你的头发是金色、红色、黑色或者棕色,或者你的肤色太白还是太黑,都与它无关。

你得了多少分,你有多聪明,别人认为你有多聪明,或者智力标准测试告诉你有多聪明,与它无关。

它不是把你各方面的情况写在一张纸上,然后看谁会"接受书面上的你",它不仅是这样。

但是,生活是关于你爱谁和伤害了谁的问题。

它是关于你故意逗谁开心或惹谁生气。

它是关于遵守诺言或者背信弃义。

它是关于友谊,把它当作一种圣洁还是利用的武器。

它是关于你所说的及其用意,也许使人痛苦,也许振奋人心。

它是关于散布谣言和捏造谈资。

它是关于你做出的判断及其原由,还有,你对谁做出的判断。

它是关于你对谁带着绝对控制和某些意图的忽视。

它是关于嫉妒、恐惧、愚昧和报复。

它是关于内心深处的恨与爱,释怀与蔓延。

但最重要的,它是关于你的生活使他人的心灵受到触动还是毒害,这样你的心不再独自悲欢。

只要你选择了触动他人的心灵,这些选择便是生活的全部。

我们该怎样给生活定义呢?过怎样的生活,只是看我们如何去安排它。不管怎样,快乐的生活才是我们生命的主题。

Life

Anonymous

Life isn't about keeping score.

It's not about how many friends you have or how accepted you are.

Not about if you have plans this weekend or if you're alone.

It isn't about who you're dating, who you used to date, how many people you've dated, or if you haven't been with anyone at all.

It isn't about who you have kissed.

It's not about sex.

It isn't about who your family is or how much money they have.

Or what kind of car you drive.

Or where you are sent to school.

It's not about how beautiful or **ugly**[1] you are.

Or what clothes you wear, what shoes you have on, or what kind of music you listen to.

It's not about if your hair is **blonde**[2], red, black, or brown or if your skin is too light or too dark.

Not about what grades you get, how smart you are, how smart everybody else thinks you are, or how smart standardized tests say you are.

It's not about representing your whole-being on a piece of paper and seeing who will "accept the written you". Life just isn't.

But, life is about who you love and who you hurt.

It's about who you make happy or unhappy purposefully.

It's about keeping or **betraying**[3] trust.

It's about friendship, used as a sanctity or a weapon.

It's about what you say and what you mean, maybe hurtful, maybe heartening.

It's about starting rumors and contributing to petty **gossip**[4].

It's about what judgments you pass and why. And who your judgment are spread to.

It's about who you've ignored with full control and intention.

It's about **jealousy**[5], fear, ignorance, and revenge.

It's about carrying inner hate and love, letting it grow, and spreading it.

But most of all, it's about using your life to touch or poison other people's hearts in such a way that could have never occurred alone.

Only you choose the way those hearts are affected, and those choices are what life's all about.

热词空间

1. ugly ['ʌgli] *adj.* 丑陋的;难看的
2. blonde [blɔnd] adj. 色白的;碧眼的
3. betray [bi'trei] *v.* 出卖;背叛
4. gossip ['gɔsip] *n.* 闲话;闲谈
5. jealousy ['dʒeləsi] *n.* 嫉妒

生活的课堂

佚名

万事皆有因，没有什么事是因巧合或运气的好坏而发生的。

疾病、伤害、情爱，曾经的荣耀和所做的傻事，都是对你灵魂的考验。如果没有这些琐碎的考验，没有疾病和各种复杂的关系，那么生活就会如同一条铺设好了却没有目的地的平坦道路。

若有人伤害你，背叛你，令你心碎，请宽恕他们！因为他们使你学会了怎样信任他人以及敞开心扉与他人沟通时谨慎的重要性。

若有人爱你，要无条件地用爱回报他们。不仅因为他们爱你，更因为他们教会你如何去爱；如何敞开心扉去感受你未曾有过的感受；如何睁开眼睛去看你未曾看到过的事物。

珍惜每一天。感激生命中的每一个瞬间，尽量从中吸取更多，因为一切都不会复返。

与你从未交谈过的人聊天吧，实际上你是去倾听，但要昂起头，这样做是你的权利。

承认自己是一个了不起的人，要自信。若你都不相信自己，别人就更不会相信你了。

你可以按自己的意愿去生活，创造你独特的生活，活出自我。

生活本身就是一个课堂，我们都是需要进修的学生，它可以教给我们许多东西。关于爱，我们是需要付出的，只要我们付出了，就不会有后悔的一天。

A Lesson in Life

Anonymous

Everything happens for a reason. Nothing happens by chance or by means of good or bad luck.

Illness[1], **injury**[2], love, lost moments of true greatness and sheer stupidity all occur to test the limits of your soul. Without these small tests, if they be events, illnesses or relationships, life would be like a smoothly paved, straight, flat road to nowhere.

If someone hurts you, betrays you, or breaks you heart, forgive them. For they have helped you learn about trust and the importance of being **cautious**[3] to who you open your heart to.

If someone loves you, love them back unconditionally, not only because they love you, but because they are teaching you to love and opening your heart and eyes to things you would have never seen or felt without them.

Make every day count. Appreciate every moment and take from it everything that you possibly can, for you may never be able to experiences it again.

Talk to people who you have never talked to before, and actually listen. Hold your head up because you have every right to.

Tell yourself you are a great individual and believe in yourself, for if you don't believe in yourself, no one else will believe in you either.

You can make of your life anything you wish. Create your own life and then go out and live.

1. illness ['ilnis] *n.* 疾病；生病
2. injury ['indʒəri] *n.* 伤害；侮辱
3. cautious ['kɔːʃəs] *adj.* 谨慎的；小心的

人生之道

佚名

要想获得成功的人生，必然需要思考。人们担心思考可能会扰乱他们的舒适和自我满足感。思考需要带着激情持之以恒地练习。激情会萌发兴趣，而兴趣又会强化思考。专注地思考有利于我们清晰地勾勒出自己头脑中最终目标的画面。

我们应该持续不断地思考。我们专心致志地思考，就能理清思路，使思维变得敏捷。学会条理清晰地思考不同事物并培养严谨的思考能力也同样重要。要激发思考力度，我们可以参加严肃的会谈或坚持自己观点的辩论，这样会迫使我们的思考更清晰、更客观。阅读书籍和杂志对于我们清晰地阐述观点也很有帮助。

对于我们接触的其他人，积极思考有巨大的影响力。而那些有效提高思考能力的人，能使自己更充实。

心灵小语

在做任何事情之前，我们都要经过一番深思熟虑，才会付诸行动，而在思考时，我们也要带着激情去联想，这是因为激情会让我们更投入，更易思考。这样我们才可以更好地实现自己的目标。

For Success in Life

Anonymous

Thinking is necessary if you want to succeed in life. People fear that thinking may upset their comfort and self-satisfaction. Thinking needs constant practice with enthusiasm. Enthusiasm generates interest and **sustains**[1] thinking. And concentration will help us form a clear picture in our minds of the **ultimate**[2] objective.

Thinking should be constant and **continuous**[3]. With concentration, we can arrange thoughts in order and become a rapid thinker. It is also important to develop organised thinking learning to think of different things one by one in order. We can stimulate thinking power by taking part in serious conversations or discussions and **defending**[4] our positions so that it will drive us to think more clearly and objectively. Reading books and magazines will also help us in the process of formulating ideas.

Positive thinking has a tremendous influence over others with whom we come into contact. People who succeed in improving their thinking power enrich themselves.

热词空间

1. sustain [səs'tein] v. 支撑；撑住；维持
2. ultimate ['ʌltimit] adj. 最后的；最终的
3. continuous [kən'tinjuəs] adj. 连续的；持续的
4. defend [di'fend] v. 防护；辩护

和自己交谈的力量

佚名

生活如同一个摇摆在快乐和悲伤之间的大秋千。当我们处于悲伤的下坡时,又开始向快乐的上坡进军。沮丧时,我们会伤心地跌入绝望之谷。能摆脱这种困境的人是战胜悲伤的胜者。

当你感觉情绪欠佳时,失落和困惑之感便会油然而生,此时是你最困难的时期,用自我交谈的方式能有效地鼓舞自己。自我交谈,事实上就是和自己说话,它能有效地探索灵魂。与自己说话时,谈话受良心的支配,使我们很难撒谎。自我交谈能有效地了解自己的想法,强烈地影响我们的思想。我们的大脑如耳朵一样会接收来自思想的信息。反复鼓舞的话语能对大脑的反应进行有效的调节。

自我交谈是一种软件,当它被适当地装入我们的思想时,便能指导我们得到好的结果并拥有健康的心态。

事实上,别人常会建议我们在学习、体育运动和生活等方面做得更好。我们总会对他们的唠叨感到厌烦,对他们建设性的意见充耳不闻,因为那些声音并非发自我们内心。若它们发自内心,我们就会全身心投入地去践行。所以说,与自己交谈能使我们的现状有所改善。

每个人都是优缺点兼而有之。我们不愿在公众面前承认,我们也知道自己个人生活的许多方面是可以做得更好的。这样"通过自我交谈能使我们趋于完善"这一观点在现实生活中得以实现。

如果你性格内向,想和邻居朋友一样成为善于交际的人,你需要做的就是和自己交谈。诚挚而满怀感情地对自己说"我能和他一样,我是个天生的演讲家。我的确喜欢人们，喜欢随心所欲地与大家畅谈。我必须时刻准备好聆听或发言。"如果你爱一个人，并想让他或她知道，那么就告诉自己"我全身心地爱她，我清楚，她是我的唯一。倘若不让她知道，这对我来说不公平。每个人都希望得到别人的爱，她也不例外。"这不过是我举的一些例子，如何去表白由你自己决定。

若你对做好一切很有信心，那没有比自我交谈更好的激励方法了。因此，开始交谈吧。

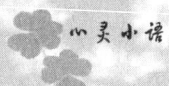

心灵小语

每当你遇到烦心事，心情郁闷时，你会用什么方法来解决呢？是任其发展，还是强迫自己克制住呢？本文所介绍的方法，无疑是一个简便又有效的解决方法——和自己交谈，把烦心事都说出来，告诉自己要提高自信，是一个自我开导！

美丽英文
Beautiful English

Power of Self-talk

Anonymous

Life is like a big **swing**[1], dangling between the depths of happiness and sadness. As soon as we descend down the slope of sadness, we **accelerate**[2] over the ever-feel-good acclivity of happiness. At times of distress, when we are down we slip over an abyss of emotional **trauma**[3] and frustrations. One who can rise above the occasion, is the architect of many wins over sorrows.

To come above tougher times you have to pep yourself up, when you are feeling low, lost and confused. This can be done effectively by self-talk. Self-talk is a way of talking to oneself. It can be effectively used for soul searching. When talking to ourselves, we hardly lie as our conscience controls our speech. Self-talk is efficient because when we are vocal about our thoughts, it makes a larger impact on our mind. Our brain then receives the same message from the mind as well as the ears. This repetition of pep talks and thoughts fine tunes the performance of the brain.

Self-talk is a software, which when properly loaded onto our mind directs ourselves for better results and a healthy mind.

Actually many times in our life, we find others advising us to do better in studies, sports, life etc. We usually get bugged by these people and blank our ears out of their constructive suggestions. It is because it doesn't come from within us. And when something comes from within you, you always try your best to do justice to it. Self-talk can thus **ameliorate**[4] our status.

Each one of us has some good points and some bad ones. Though we hardly admit in public, we know in our mind that we could do better in some areas of our personal landscape. This get better attitude can be converted into a practical reality using self-talk.

If you are an **introvert**[5] and you want to be the gregarious person like your friend next door, all you need to do is talk to yourself. Tell yourself with all the sincerity and emotions that "I can be like him. I am a natural born speaker. I do like people and speaking comes naturally to me. I just have to be ready to listen and speak". Suppose you love a person and want to tell him or her, then just say to yourselves "I love her with all my heart. She is the only one and I know it. If I don't let her know, it would be grave injustice on my part. Every person loves to be loved. Even she will". These are just some examples I have explained. It's up to you to program your own **mantra**[6].

If you are highly optimistic to do better, there is no better motivator than self-talk. So guys start talking.

1. swing [swiŋ] *n.* 秋千
2. accelerate [æk'seləreit] *v.* 加速；促进
3. trauma ['trɔːmə] *n.* [医] 外伤；损伤
4. ameliorate [ə'miːljəreit] *v.* 改善；改进
5. introvert [ˌintrəu'vəːt] *n.* 性格内向的人
6. mantra ['mʌntrə] *n.* 颂歌

美丽英文
Beautiful English

重新定义自己

佚名

你是怎样定义自己的?一位母亲、女儿、妻子、朋友、丈夫、儿子、老师、学生、律师、会计师,还是其他什么头衔呢?或者你是根据别人对你的感觉而给自己下定义?这些定义的依据与你的学识、个人经历和本质有何相似之处吗?

在你静心独处之时,在无法言说的快乐之中,你是否有一种无法抵抗的神勇之感——那是一种战无不胜、攻无不克的感觉——若你倾心投入,可以完成任何事情的感觉。这种感觉并不是随意就能产生的。

是什么妨碍了你神圣力量的发挥呢?

试想,一个有天然磁性的铁棒,其固有的磁性能使其对别的物体产生吸引或排斥。但时间久了,铁棒就会生锈,磁力便开始逐渐消失。磁体无法抵制外界环境对其的氧化作用,磁力最终失效。这并不是意味着铁棒不具有潜在的原始磁力,只是需要将锈渍除掉而已。或者你也可以想象一个亮着的灯泡,上面罩了一层煤灰,若煤灰不除,灯泡就永远无法实现其照亮的功效。

根据古代的梵文记载,类似的现象也曾出现在人类的历程中。一种天生的无穷能量蕴含在每个人身上,若进行错误的引导,就不能淋漓尽致地将其发挥出来。生活方式、环境污染和各方面的压力都妨碍了我们潜能的发挥。

挽救的方法是:调节生活方式,有效地应付压力,使生活有侧重点。其措施包括:

熟悉你所吃的和所用的对自己及环境的影响。选择自然和有机的产品而用。

对生活要怀有善意、关怀和慈善之心,这有利于维持你在生活中的中心位置,保持与源极的感应。你心中的无尽源泉就是你的发电站。

不要妄加评论人和环境,理性地拥抱生活的每一时刻,因为一切可能都蕴藏其中。

你的真实本性是强大无敌的,要在练习瑜伽和沉思默想中去体悟。

一旦触及到了自己的真实本性,你就将无所不能——因为你确切地定义了自己,便会拥有真正的力量。

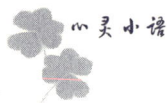
心灵小语

人们会被自己的多个头衔弄糊涂,分不清哪个才是真正的自己。人们需要时常定义自己,确切地定义自己,告诉自己的身份究竟是什么,自己该做些什么,这样就会拥有真正的力量去做好每一件事。

Redefine Yourself

Anonymous

How do you define yourself? As a mother, daughter, wife, friend, husband, son, teacher, student, lawyer, accountant, or any one of a **myriad**[1] different titles? Or do you define yourself by others' **perception**[2] of you? Do any of these come close to your own knowledge, your personal experience of whom you really are?

In your quiet moments, in times of inexplicable joy, have you had the overwhelming and yet clear and **lucid**[3] feeling of total invincibility—a feeling that nothing can hold you down, that you can accomplish anything and everything if you put your mind to it? Well, that feeling is not a random one.

What is it that gets in the way of your **exquisite**[4] power?

Consider for a moment an iron bar that has magnetic power inherently in it. It will attract or repel things based on it's own **intrinsic**[5] magnetism. Over time, if this bar begins to rust, its power will begin to diminish. The oxidative damage from the environment that the magnet has not been able to resist, will render it ineffective, eventually. This in no way means the iron bar is not capable of its latent, original power. All it needs to do is shed its rust. Or, consider if you will, a light bulb that is lit, but covered with soot. As long as the soot remains, it will be unable to fulfill the very purpose it was meant to serve to radiate light.

According to ancient Vedic texts, this is in effect what happens to the human experience. The infinite power that is naturally present in each and every one of us by virtue of our own consciousness, can be rendered ineffective if not tended to properly. The stress of our lifestyle, the pollution of our environment, and the collective stress of our world keeps us from functioning at our full potential.

But there are remedies: incorporate modalities in your lifestyle that effectively combat stress and help keep you centered. Some of these options are:

Be aware of what you eat, and what you use—both on yourself, and in your environment. Choose natural, organic products.

Live a life of kindness, compassion, and charity—it keeps you connected to your center, your source, that infinite **reservoir**[6] within you that is your powerhouse.

Don't judge people, or situations—approach each moment with the knowledge that it contains within it the potential of any number of possibilities.

To connect with your real nature that is unbounded and **invincible**[7], practice yoga and meditation.

Once you are in touch with your true nature, then nothing is beyond your means—you are truly empowered. And THAT is an accurate definition of YOU!

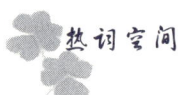 热词空间

1. myriad ['miriəd] *adj.* 无数的；一万的；种种的
2. perception [pə'sepʃən] *n.* 理解；感觉
3. lucid ['luːsid] *adj.* 明晰的
4. exquisite ['ekskwizit] *adj.* 优美的；高雅的
5. intrinsic [in'trinsik] *adj.* （指价值、性质）固有的；内在的
6. reservoir ['rezəvwaː] *n.* 水库；蓄水池
7. invincible [in'vinsəbl] *adj.* 不能征服的；无敌的

聆听心灵

佚名

从你被带到这个世上的那刻起,便开始聆听自己的心灵。最初两年你不会说话,只能用心去感悟万事万物。

心灵之声是人的潜意识的表达。潜意识总是人的思想观念的二级反映,它评判着世间的是非曲直。当我们违背内心的意愿做了某事时,就会有负罪感,且一生都会为之困扰。

在我们情绪低落或难以忘却那些令自己失望的时刻时,我们需要某种情感和智力支持。我们通常会在最悲伤的时候,向最亲密的朋友和最亲爱的家人倾诉,以减轻精神负担。因为有了支持的听众,我们就可以克服不安和焦躁的情绪。心灵让我们把所有烦恼都埋藏到记忆深处,这样我们会很快恢复活力。

多数时候我们的心灵都是对的,因为它比任何人,甚至比我们更了解自己。它是直觉这个魔鬼的孩子,自小时起,就一直伴随我们。大多时候跟着直觉走是有益的,因为它是我们智力和体力的同步回应。

当你试着吸第一支烟时,当你必须在一场辩论中支持一方时,总会觉得有些为难。此时,心灵会自然得出结论,毫不夸张地说,它会为我们以后的生活撒下不愉快的种子。当所有这些问题都出现时,我们要么忽略内心的士气鼓动者,要么融入这个世界,去找寻精神领袖和快乐源泉。

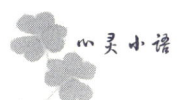

你曾经静静地聆听过自己的心灵吗?你读得懂它吗?心灵之声是我们的内心所想。如果我们做了某件事情,心灵的反应会直接表达我们的内心所想,因为它是人类思想观念的二级反映。

Listen to Your Inner Voice

Anonymous

Very much, ever since you were brought into this world. When you couldn't open your mouth till the first two years on planet earth, inner voice is the one through which you interpreted and understood things.

Inner voice is the voice mouth of the subconscious mind. The subconscious mind is always acting as a secondary reflector of thoughts and ideas in the body. It justifies and rationalizes what is right and what is wrong. When we go against what the inner voice says we get a guilty conscious and are bothered by it throughout our lives.

At times when we are feeling low or those unforgettable moments when we are let down, we seem to need some kind of emotional or mental support. We usually speak to our closest pal or our dearest family member during times of distress to ease the burden. At such times we get over the initial drizzle of emotional anxiety and mental restlessness, because of the pepping up by our empathic listener. We suddenly feel rejuvenated because our inner voice alerts us to get on with things and leave the things of past on the memory books of our brain.

The inner voice is always right most of the times because it knows us better than others and probably even ourselves. It is the dare devil child of the intuitions which we have been having since childhood.It's good to go by intuitions most of the times because it's the response provided due to the synchronism between our mental and physical being.

Whenever you are trying your first cigarette, or whenever you are asked to take sides in an argument, you are always in a sense of dilemma. During these times your inner voice automatically gives its verdict, which when over written, might leave us unhappy in the future. It's up to us to either ignore the morale booster inside us or go out to the world and search for spiritual guru's and happiness, when all these things are very much present within us.

美丽英文
Beautiful English

打造自己的生活

佚名

每个人都在创造着自己的生活。拥有自己的生活是你的绝对权利。然而,人们总是否认自己拥有描绘所渴望的生活的能力,他们忽视了这样一个最根本的真理:决定我们成败的不是外部环境,而是我们内心深处的自我信念和创造我们最想得到的生活的意愿。

显然,这里的挑战是创造和拥有你自己的真实生活。当你开始过着自己的生活,认识到怎样去营造完全取决于自己时,你就能根据自己的选择和渴望来设计生活。你会在这里学到一些东西,比如责任和无限,他们将会指引你打造自己想要的生活。这些启示将会赋予你打造生活所必需的基本工具。

承担责任意味着承担义务,并承认你对环境的影响和你在环境中的角色。它意味着你要对自己的行为负责,并完全接受你的行为所导致的一切后果。

承担责任将会促使你不断前进,直到实现更大的目标。我认识一个叫玛丽的女士,她对自己负责的故事一直鼓舞着我。玛丽出生在古巴,两岁时和全家一起搬到迈阿密。他们住在迈阿密最危险的贫困区,那里每天都充斥着犯罪和吸毒。然而,玛丽年仅八岁时,就决定打造自己的生活,不走当女仆或在当地做超市收银员的老路。于是,她每天去上学,有时候不得不跨过门口的醉汉,只有这样她才能接受教育,过上更好的生活。

玛丽最终离开了迈阿密,受到了很好的教育,并开发了自身在音乐方面的潜力。她本可以屈从于生来注定的命运,或者一味埋怨她的父母和所处的环境;她也可以拒绝对当前的情形负责。但是,她却对自己负责,打造了能引以为豪的生活。责任是成年人的主修课,如果你还没有学会这堂课,现在还不晚。记住,生活会赐予你足够多的机会让你完全学懂。

无限,你最后必须学会的课程是无限,它是一种你去成就自我或创造生活时没有任何束缚的感觉。当你懂得自己的发展永无止境、潜能无穷无尽时,便学会了这门课。

你生下来便知道自己的潜能。可是,当你长大成为社会中的一员,你可能会开始相信,有太多的限定阻碍你实现最高的精神、情感或智力进展。然而,限定只存于你的心里。当你能超越他们的时候,你就学会了无限这一课。

我孩提时的一位老师深谙无限的重要性。她每天都提醒我们,无论多么艰难,只要用心,我们就能成就任何事。我衷心地希望世界上的每一个学校都有一位像卡波恩夫人这样的老师,那样,我们的孩子就能知道自身的潜力,并努力去挖掘。世界上,无数的人都证明了这个道理:世上无难事,只怕有心人。

当你开始过着自己的生活,认识到怎样去营造完全取决于自己时,你就能根据自己的选择和渴望来设计生活。自己的生活要靠自己来创造,没有人可以替代我们去做我们想做的事。我们是独一无二的,无可替代的,我们要用自己的独特性,打造属于自己的生活。

How to Build Your Life

Anonymous

Every person creates his or her own reality. Authorship of your life is one of your absolute rights; yet so often people **deny**[1] that they have the ability to script the life they desire. They look past the fundamental truth that it is not our external resources that determine our success or failure, but rather our own belief in ourselves and our willingness to create a life according to our highest **aspirations**[2].

Clearly, the challenge here is to create and own your own reality. When you begin to live your life understanding that what you make of it is up to you, you are able to design it according to your authentic choices and desires. You will learn lessons here, such as responsibility and limitlessness, which will lead you to the life you were meant to live. These lessons provide you with the essential tools you need in order to take command of your life.

To take responsibility means you admit your accountability and acknowledge your influence and role in the circumstances in which you find yourself. It means you are answerable for your behavior and you fully accept any consequences created by your actions.

To take responsibility will propel you forward and onward to your greater good. I know of a woman named Mary whose story of personal responsibility has always inspired me. Mary was born in Cuba and moved to Miami with her family when she was two years old. They lived in terrible poverty in a dangerous part of the city, where crime and drugs were part of everyday life. Mary was determined, however, even at the young age of eight, to make something of her life other than follow the expected route of becoming a **maid**[3], or a **cashier**[4] at the local supermarket. So she got herself to school each and every day, sometimes having to step over drunks passed out in the doorway, just so she could get education and give herself a better life.

Mary eventually left Miami, obtained a good education, and fostered her natural music ability. Mary could have given in to the life she was born into, or remained mired in blaming her parents and culture for her circumstances. She could have refused to take responsibility for the situation. Instead, however, Mary took responsibility for herself and created a life of which she can be proud.

Responsibility is a major lesson of adulthood. If you still haven't learned the lesson of responsibility, it's not too late. Remember, life will provide you with plenty of opportunities to get it right.

Limitlessness, the final lesson you must learn is limitlessness, it is the sense that there are no boundaries to what you can become or do. You learn it when you know that your evolution is never-ending and your potential for growth reaches to infinity.

You were born knowing your limitlessness. As you grew and became socialized in this world, however, you might have come to believe that there are boundaries that prevent you from reaching the highest levels of spiritual, emotional, or mental evolution. However, boundaries exist only in your mind. When you are able to transcend them, you learn the lesson of limitlessness.

When I was young, I had a teacher who understood the importance of this lesson. She reminded us every day that we could do anything we set our minds to, no matter how impossible it might seem or how strong the opposition is. It is my sincere hope that there is a teacher like Mrs. Carbene in every school around the world, so that our children can know the wonder and power they have within themselves and will strive to access it. In this world, we have countless people who have proven that a person can do whatever he or she strives to do.

热词空间

1. deny [di'nai] v. 否认；拒绝
2. aspiration [ˌæspə'reiʃən] n. 热望；渴望
3. maid [meid] n. 少女；女仆
4. cashier [kə'ʃiə] n. 出纳员；司库

生活半对半

佚名

我信奉生活半对半的理论。一半比常态更美好，另一半则会更糟糕。我觉得，生活就像钟摆一样会来回晃动。我们需要时间和阅历才能懂得生活的常态，也正是这样，我懂得了如何处变不惊地面对未来的一切。

让我们以这些参数为基点来思考：是的，我注定会死去。我已经历了如此多的死亡：父母、友人、受人爱戴的老板，还有心爱的宠物。这些死亡当中，有些突如其来，直击眼前；有些却是缓慢地折磨着，令人苦不堪言。糟糕的事隐藏在心底最深处。

然而，生活中也有这样辉煌的时候：与心爱的人坠入爱河并喜结良缘；养育孩子，做些父亲该做的事，如训练我儿子的棒球队；当儿子带着狗在小溪里游泳时，自己在一旁荡桨泛舟，我发现他的同情心是如此强烈——对蜗牛也表现出友爱；他的想象力是如此活跃——即使是一堆零散的积木，他也能造出太空飞船来。

但是，人生中有一片辽阔的草地。各种好事坏事都在那里戏剧般地颠倒浮沉。这使我确信了生活半对半的理论。

有一年春天，我过早种下了玉米，那里地势低洼，容易被洪水淹没。因此，我受到邻居们的嘲笑，也为自己的努力白白浪费而懊恼不已。那年夏天异常酷热——我生命中最可怕的热浪和干旱降临：空调坏了、水井干涸了、婚姻结束了、工作丢了、钱也没了。我的生活如同一首乡村歌曲所描绘的情节——我讨厌乡村音乐。唯一使我精神振奋的，是一支人气攀升的堪萨斯皇家棒球队，它将首次出征世界大赛了。

回想那个可怕的夏天，我很快明白，祸福相依，不顺心的事情总会过去。我要拥有和享受宁静的时光，它们使我振作起来，敢于面对突如其来的意外事件，确保我再度辉煌起来。我的皇家棒球队最近陷入低迷状态时，半对半理论甚至帮助我看到了希望。这是新手们艰难奋斗的领域，这样，几年后，我们就可以收获金秋十月。

哦，对了，玉米的收成？因为那个酷暑，地上的湿度恰到好处，种植过早使得授粉期避开了酷热当头时,而稀少的雨水使挺立的玉米免受洪水之灾。那年冬天,玉米堆满了我的谷仓——每株玉米秆上结了三个硕大饱满的玉米棒,每一个棒子都长满了玉米粒——邻居们的地里只有褐色干瘪的壳。

尽管以前种玉米,总没什么收成,将来可能还会如此,但我仍要继续种下去,因为这经历了旱季依然能丰收的玉米大大鼓舞了我。

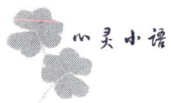

不论昨天的一切是好是坏,我们都应该把它忘记,并满怀信心地迎接新一轮太阳的升起,因为只要坚持就一定会成功。不论我们曾经是否罪孽深重,在将来的道路上,我们不应就此沉沦,而是要努力克服,做到更好!

The 50-Percent Theory of Life

Anonymous

I believe in the 50-percent theory. Half the time things are better than normal; the other half, they are worse. I believe life is a **pendulum**[1] swing. It takes time and experience to understand what normal is, and that gives me the perspective to deal with the surprises of the future.

Let's **benchmark**[1] the parameters: Yes, I will die. I've dealt with the deaths of both parents, a best friend, a beloved boss and cherished pets. Some of these deaths have been violent, before my eyes, or slow and agonizing. Bad stuff, and it belongs at the bottom of the scale.

Then there are those high points: romance and marriage to the right person; having a child and doing those Dad things like coaching my son's baseball team, paddling around the creek in the boat while he's swimming with the dogs, discovering his compassion so deep it manifests even in his kindness to snails, his imagination so vivid he builds a spaceship from a scattered pile of Legos.

But there is a vast meadow of life in the middle, where the bad and the good flip-flop acrobatically. This is what convinces me to believe in the 50-percent theory.

One spring I planted corn too early in a bottomland so flood-prone that neighbors laughed. I felt chagrined at the wasted effort. Summer turned brutal—the worst heat wave and drought in my lifetime. The air-conditioner died, the well went dry, the marriage ended, the job lost, the money gone. I was living lyrics from a country tune—music I **loathed**[3]. Only a surging Kansas City Royals team, bound for their first World Series, **buoyed**[4] my spirits.

Looking back on that horrible summer, I soon understood that all succeeding good things merely offset the bad. Worse than normal wouldn't last long. I am owed and savor the **halcyon**[5] times. They reinvigorate me for the next nasty surprise and offer assurance that I can thrive. The 50 percent theory even helps me see hope beyond my Royals' recent slump, a field of struggling rookies sown so that some year soon we can reap an October harvest.

Oh, yeah, the corn crop? For that one blistering summer, the ground moisture was just right, planting early allowed pollination before heat withered the tops, and the lack of rain spared the standing corn from floods. That winter my crib overflowed with corn—fat, healthy three-to-a-stalk ears filled with kernels from heel to tip—while my neighbors' fields yielded only brown, empty husks.

Although plantings past may have fallen below the 50-percent expectation, and they probably will again in the future, I am still sustained by the crop that flourishes during the drought.

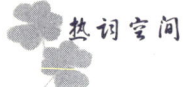

热词空间

1. pendulum ['pendjuləm] *n.* 钟摆；摇锤
2. benchmark [bentʃ'maːk] *n.* [计]基准
3. loath [ləuθ] *adj.* 不情愿的；勉强的
4. buoy [bɔi] *v.* 使浮起；支撑；鼓励
5. halcyon ['hælsiən] *adj.* 平静的；太平的